DADDY'S
MONEY

ALAN CHIN

Dreamspinner Press

Published by
Dreamspinner Press
5032 Capital Circle SW
Ste 2, PMB# 279
Tallahassee, FL 32305-7886
USA
http://www.dreamspinnerpress.com/

Daddy's Money

Cover Art by L.C. Chase
http://www.lcchase.com

ISBN: 978-1-62380-232-5

Printed in the United States of America
First Edition
December 2012

eBook edition available
eBook ISBN: 978-1-62380-233-2

Praise for ALAN CHIN

Match Maker

"In a word ... Wow! After reading his previous two novels, I expect outstanding writing from Mr. Chin, but this raises the bar far above any expectations I had."

— Bob Lind, *Echo* magazine

"This beautiful story is one that will haunt me, and which I will hold close for a very long time."

—Reviews by Amos Lassen

"In tennis vernacular, *Match Maker* is an 'Ace'."

—eBook Addict Reviews

The Lonely War

"I found it a truthful telling of one man's life and a faithful account of the war in Asia. I also found a love story that will stay with me long after the last page has been read. I fell in love with all these brave men and I wish them well wherever they might land."

—Speak Its Name

Island Song

"A beautiful book. The real crime here would be in not reading it."

—Victor J. Banis, author

Butterfly's Child

"It's a beautiful story and one I'd recommend."

—Long and Short Reviews

http://www.dreamspinnerpress.com

By ALAN CHIN

NOVELS
Butterfly's Child
Daddy's Money
Island Song
Match Maker
The Lonely War

EBOOKS
Haji's Exile
Simple Treasures

Published by DREAMSPINNER PRESS
http://www.dreamspinnerpress.com

CHAPTER ONE

HE ROLLED over and nuzzled his pillow. Through the thin membrane of his unconscious, he saw not the pillow, but mounds of coppery flesh, sweaty and firm, and appropriately stimulating. He could not see a face on this nameless form because he concentrated only on those luscious, satiny curves. His lips sought out that moist crevice he knew would bring them both the most pleasure. A smile creased his lips as he kneaded his face into white linen, kissing its softness, inhaling the fresh scent of a spring morning, but a noise drew his awareness up from the depths of his tantalizing vision. Beyond the borders of his dream, barely noticeable but growing louder, he heard the pulse of an alarm clock.

His eyelids fluttered and one opened. Sunlight poured through a window like melted butter, spilling onto his face, making him squint. The combination of warm rays and cool breeze drifting through the open window pampered his face. It felt strange to lie in the sun, smelling sweet scents that permeated the air. Through the yellow glare, he saw the flashing red diodes of a clock—7:00.

His first reaction—a deep feeling of loss and a desire to return to the satiny skin he had been kissing—fled after a second, expanding into a moment of wonder. He became caught, as often happened, in that void where his consciousness was aware but his identity—his personal history—had not yet reentered his body. He lay staring at the clock, feeling the sunlight warming his face, wondering where he was, and more importantly, who he was. Now with both eyes open, he lifted his head and scanned the room, searching for clues to his identity.

Books, posters, computer gear, and general clutter gave the impression of a classic frat-house bedroom, one vaguely familiar. He read the spines of books standing at attention on the shelf— Sartre, Camus, Graham Greene, Thoreau, Isherwood, Maugham, and Mary Renault's *The Persian Boy*. His eyes rested on a name scribbled on a notebook lying on the floor near his bed: Sayen Hommet. The name meant nothing to him. Then his gaze shifted to a small silk prayer rug, the intricately patterned rug his own mother had woven at their family loom in Tripoli and given to him at his circumcision. In a flash, his memory ignited and his personal history crashed down on him, a millstone crushing his chest to the point he strained to breathe.

Yes, he thought, *Sayen Hommet, medical student, Muslim.* After ten years of living in this country of unbelievers, he still had these problems waking up because he simply could not adapt to days not measured out by the shrill calls of the muezzin. He had owned a watch with an alarm set to mark all the hours of prayer, but he had pawned it a year ago. He glanced at the clock again and realized he was much more than a Muslim medical student—he was late!

He leaped from his bed and ripped open the top drawer of his bureau, searching for clean underwear. Moments later he bounced across the room on one leg, pulling on loose-fitting slacks while at the same time running an electric razor over his face. There were no clean shirts in the closet. He dashed to a pile of clothes on the floor and lifted a shirt to his face, sniffing. He threw it aside and lifted another shirt, which smelled worse than the first one. He lifted a third and slipped it on, not bothering to smell it. He stepped into a pair of loafers and raced out the doorway and down the hall to the bathroom where he meticulously washed his hands, feet, and face at a sink. After returning to his room, he kicked off his shoes and stood before his prayer rug, which lay along an axis facing holy Mecca.

Allahu Akbar, Allahu Akbar—God is great. He sank to his knees, bowing into the first prostration. "I bear witness that there is no God but God, and Muhammad is the messenger of God." His deep voice murmured like the rumbling of distant thunder. Within the room's stillness, the air trembled, making the light shimmer. "God is great, the merciful, the compassionate." He could feel the blood circulating through his body as he opened himself to the universe and let God flow into—or perhaps out of, he was never sure which—his being. "There is no God but God." Now came the part he loved most, that feeling of oneness with the Almighty, joining with the pulsating energy that binds all things together. His mind floated in a sphere of calm wonder. Eyes closed, breathing from deep within his diaphragm, he felt his soul smile.

Moments later, a rap on the door and a harsh voice ruptured his bliss. "Hom, get it in gear. You're late again!"

Sayen dipped his forehead to the rug once more before jumping to his feet. He donned a white lab coat, slipped into his shoes, and grabbed his backpack before racing out the doorway and down the stairs.

Seven frat brothers huddled around a table eating breakfast. Doug Housman slathered butter over his toast, added a generous helping of grape jelly, and brought it to his mouth at the instant Sayen dashed through the kitchen, speeding toward the back door. Sayen grabbed Doug's toast as he flew by, and crammed it into his mouth as he burst out the doorway.

"Hey, bitch," Doug screamed after him, "where's the fifty bucks you owe me?"

Sayen sprinted to the curb where he always parked his Austin Mini Cooper, but he stopped cold before he reached the sidewalk. Before him, a yellow tow truck lifted the front end of his Mini off the pavement. "Hey, that's my car."

The tow-truck driver leaned out of the cab. "Was your car. Now it's the bank's."

"What the hell am I supposed to do now?" Sayen said to nobody in particular. He studied the driver, a bear of a man with a grease smudge slashed across his cheek, wondering if anything could persuade him to lower the vehicle. The brute was too big to threaten, and Sayen had no cash for a bribe.

"Pay your bills," the driver snarled.

The truck jerked away from the curb and sped down the street. Sayen threw his hands in the air. "With what?" he yelled. "Do you have any idea how much Stanford tuition costs!"

Three minutes later, Sayen raced across campus on a borrowed skateboard. He recklessly dashed between fast-moving cars, bumped one student who dropped her books and screamed expletives, and almost ran down a toddler. He flew all out, heedless of oncoming danger or the carnage he left behind.

CAMPBELL REARDON watched a woman's face, red and dripping with sweat, scrunch into a mask of pure agony. Her breathing became loud, frantic, crescendoing into a scream. "Oh God! What's happening?" Her panting accelerated, wet sobbing breaths on the verge of hyperventilation. She leaned back on the table with a sheet draped over her elevated knees.

Her husband held her hand, stroking her forehead. "Breathe, sweetheart. Concentrate."

The woman's moans built into another scream.

On the far side of the room, Nurse Peggy Warren prepared bathwater and blankets. She had a bird's narrow lips, bottle-red hair with forties-era bangs, and a Carolina accent that always sounded slightly pretentious. Beside Campbell, crusty old Dr. Crill studied his wristwatch, timing the pains. Campbell was feeling his usual sting of resentment that came whenever he had to work with Dr. Crill. *The dinosaur should have retired when I was in diapers.* He was convinced that the reason Crill treated him with disdain was not the fact that he was a handsome twenty-six-year-old with wavy blond hair, perfect teeth, and brimming with life, but rather that everything about Campbell spelled money—manners, posture, grooming. Everything except the nervous expression he could feel on his face at that moment.

"Late again," Crill snapped. "How many times have I warned him?"

Crill glared at Campbell with hard, unfathomable eyes until good manners forced Campbell to look away. He turned his head to stare out a bank of windows overlooking Stanford campus, but what caught his attention was a moth with squiggly yellow markings on its wings battering itself against the inside of the windowpane.

"I'm sure he's only moments away, Dr. Crill." Campbell continued to watch the moth, somehow hoping it would find a way back outside, to break free and ride the wind. He yearned for a miracle, and he knew that his desire had more to do with Sayen than the moth.

The woman in labor screamed again as agony arched her back off the table.

"Be strong, sweetheart," her husband crooned. "Breathe deeply."

She reached up and slapped her husband's face once, twice. She tried for a hat trick, but he pulled out of her reach. "Don't tell me to breathe, you turd—*Do something*! Make them give me the fucking shot!"

"We have plenty of time here," Dr. Crill said to Campbell. "I'll be at the nurse's station checking on other patients. Send the nurse for me if the baby crowns."

Campbell nodded.

"And Campbell, if Sayen is not here by the time I return, I'm washing him out of the program. We take medicine seriously on this campus, and that means showing up on time, every time."

"We don't know what's keeping him," Campbell snapped, his anger leaping into the red zone. "It could be an emergency."

The expression on Crill's face revealed he did not like the tone the conversation had taken. He closed his eyes, obviously trying to determine if he was overreacting. "What do you think he'd prefer, Campbell, washing out of the program or setting him back a year?"

Campbell turned his attention to the windows. The moth still battered itself against the glass. "Are those the only choices, killing his dream or throwing him deeper into debt and delaying graduation by a year? Well, thanks. I'm sure he'll be humbled with gratitude."

Crill's eyes narrowed as they followed Campbell's stare to the window. "As well he should be. Few people get to choose." He stood silent, no doubt waiting for a proper, reverential response. When none came, he said, "Very well."

Crill picked up a pad of paper from a nearby table, strolled to the window, lifted the pad, and smashed the moth.

Campbell willed his face into neutral as his anger turned into shame, which stemmed less from ingratitude than from the dangerous way he had allowed himself to reveal his contempt when it could have been so easily concealed. That was a weakness that could get him drummed out of medical school, and he vowed never to allow himself that response again. His only hope of becoming a doctor was to placate Crill and all the other arrogant bastards like him in a self-effacing manner. *And that I will do, no matter what.*

Campbell's chest squeezed tight. His lungs labored and his eyes watered. He reached into his pocket for his inhaler and lifted it to his mouth. One squirt brought sweet relief, and that helped calm him.

As Dr. Crill breezed out the doorway, another wave of pain rocked the patient. She grabbed her husband by the shirt collar and squeezed. He fought to suck air into his lungs. As the pain rolled away, the husband pulled back, gasping for breath. He staggered to Campbell and clutched his arm. "Doc, you gotta give her that shot."

Campbell glanced at the doorway, thinking he should probably go after Crill, but clearly not wanting to. "I wish I could, Mr. Bishop, but I'm a student here. I'm not allowed to administer drugs without a doctor's supervision."

"There must be something you can do. I mean, look at her. She's in agony!"

Mr. Bishop clenched Campbell's arm so tight he was in pain himself. Campbell could feel beads of sweat breaking onto his forehead. "Dr. Crill will be back any second. As soon as he's here, I'll administer the shot. I promise."

Another scream sent Mr. Bishop back to his wife's side to dab her forehead with a damp cloth.

Nurse Peggy turned on Campbell like an attack dog. "Her pains are under a minute. I'll get Dr. Crill."

Campbell rushed to put himself between Nurse Peggy and the door. He held out a hand to stop her. "We have to wait for Sayen," he choked. He gave himself another blast from his inhaler.

The patient's groans were constant. Her screams grew razor sharp. "Please, doc," Mr. Bishop pleaded, "do something."

"I'm not making that poor woman suffer another second," Nurse Peggy snapped.

"Peggy, no. Please don't!"

"Screw Sayen!" She hurled past Campbell and jerked open the door, but then froze and stared into the corridor. Campbell cocked his head to the left so he could see out the doorway, and what seemed to fill the long hallway was Sayen on his skateboard, flying toward them like a charging bull.

"Hold the door," Sayen yelled only moments before he rocketed into the delivery room. He leaned back on the board, screeching to a halt, then popped the board up and caught it with expert-like ease.

Sayen returned Nurse Peggy's glare as the ends of his mouth lifted. "Hey, Pickles, you look more sour every time I see you. Lighten up and enjoy life."

"Stop calling me that."

Campbell stepped close to Sayen, and as he did, he felt that familiar weakness come to his chest, that feeling of awkwardness he always felt around this beautiful man. Sayen had a long face, bushy eyebrows suspended above deep-set eyes, the suggestion of a moustache set over impossibly thin lips, and a prominent Adam's apple that constantly battled against his starched collar. "Crill is ready to wash you out. I've been stalling for time."

Sayen grabbed Campbell's wrist and turned it to check the face on Campbell's Rolex. "I'm exactly on time."

Campbell felt the heat from Sayen's fingers on his wrist. He was always amazed at how this lovely man generated so much energy, as if he held an entire universe of burning life deep within, a brilliant comet streaking across an empty sky. "On time for Crill means ten minutes early. You know that."

Another scream from the patient sent Nurse Peggy hurrying out the doorway.

"We both know that decrepit boob can't even see his watch," Sayen spat. "This has nothing to do with being late, and everything to do with him being a homophobic swine."

"No argument there." Yes, Campbell knew the truth of it all too well, and he felt a wave of admiration for this Muslim man who had the courage to be completely out. He also felt a tiny twinge of shame for not having the same pluck. In Sayen's excited state, he had yet to let go of Campbell's wrist. "If you're timing my pulse, let me assure you, now that you're here my heart rate has doubled."

Sayen dropped Campbell's arm. "We better scrub up before Pickles comes back dragging that knuckle scraper."

They walked to the sink, rolled up the sleeves of their lab coats, and, side by side, soaped and scrubbed. Campbell felt waves of coziness. He seldom had the chance to be this close to Sayen. He could feel the energy radiating from him, and that warm strength comforted him. He nudged closer, but Sayen moved farther away.

"Have dinner with me tonight," Campbell said in a low voice.

Sayen glanced up, lifting one eyebrow. "You know I'm in a relationship."

"Ah yes, the mystery man. Nobody believes he's real."

Sayen rinsed his hands. "He's real, alright. He just travels in different social circles."

"He's married?"

"Fuck off." Sayen grabbed a towel and dried his hands. He turned his back on Campbell and slipped on rubber gloves.

Campbell cast his towel aside and lifted a glove. "I'd show you off regardless if I had a wife. Don't you think you deserve better than that?" He stared into Sayen's eyes. It never failed to amaze him that a man of North African ancestry, with thick, jet-black hair on his head and fine hair covering his arms, would have eyes the color of the sea. But then a purple spot below Sayen's lips caught his attention. "You have a smudge of jam on your chin."

Sayen held up his gloved hands, hesitating. Campbell felt a burning desire to lean forward and lick that sweet jelly off that bronzed skin, but instead he pulled a white monogrammed handkerchief from his pocket, cleaned Sayen's chin, and slipped the handkerchief into Sayen's pocket. He smiled. "Keep it."

Sayen hesitated again until Campbell said, "It's only a hankie, not an engagement ring." Sayen dropped his head and nodded. He glanced at the patient, at her spread legs. His head jerked back to Campbell, and a mask of panic etched his face.

"What's wrong?" Campbell whispered.

"That's my undergraduate-English teacher, Mrs. Bishop. Jesus, I can't do this." He pulled the white handkerchief from his pocket and dabbed his forehead, leaving a faint line of purple.

In the three years that Campbell had known Sayen, this was the first time he had ever seen the man so unnerved. He laid a calming hand at the back of Sayen's neck, gentling him like an unbroken colt. "I thought you'd jump at the chance to rip the guts out of a homophobic Bishop."

"This is no joke. She and I were really close. I can't deal with her like this."

"You can't walk away from the people you care for, Sayen. She's a woman in pain, and we're going to help her bring new life into the world. Just focus on the baby."

Sayen glanced at her spread legs again as sweat beaded on his forehead. "Shit, it's crowning. What should we do?"

Campbell shrugged. "You're going to deliver a baby, what else?" He walked to the patient's spread legs and lifted the sheet higher. He moved to Mrs. Bishop's side and took her hand. He nodded to the husband and then to her. "Looks like someone is anxious to see its parents. It won't be long now."

NURSE PEGGY dashed to Dr. Crill, who leaned against the nurses' station counter with a cell phone pressed to his ear. "Doctor, it's time. You're needed in Delivery."

Dr. Crill held up a hand to silence her. "Yes, that's right," he said into the phone. "Sell my entire holdings in Apple. Buy ten thousand shares of IBM at market."

"Dr. Crill—"

He shushed her, turning his back to her.

Nurse Peggy folded her arms over her chest and tapped her foot. Crill paid her not the least bit of attention. "Dr. Crill, there is a patient in pain."

Crill placed his hand over the phone. "Just a damned minute, young lady."

GLOVED and masked, Sayen advanced on Mrs. Bishop's spread legs, but then he froze.

Campbell, aware that his friend's distress had deepened, came to his aid. "What now?"

"There's blood oozing out."

"For Christsake, move over." Campbell shoved Sayen aside and bent between the patient's legs. Mrs. Bishop's constant cries could shatter glass, but Campbell stayed calm, working to support the baby's head as the tiny body emerged into the world. "Mrs. Bishop, I need you to push now. Push as hard as you can."

Sayen turned away as more blood appeared. He continued to dab his face with the handkerchief, which became completely damp.

"You owe me dinner for this," Campbell said over his shoulder, "and I'm hungry for sushi."

Sayen leaned over the sink but managed to hold his stomach down. He glanced up at his image in the mirror and visibly tried to pull himself together. "You know I can't afford sushi. How about Mickey D's?"

Campbell shook his head, secretly pleased that he had gotten a dinner commitment out of this lovely man. "My dime. Sushi To Die For on 3rd Avenue, seven thirty. And don't be late."

Campbell pulled the baby away from the mother. "It's a girl, Mrs. Bishop," he said, holding it up for the parents to see.

Campbell held the infant while Sayen cut and tied the cord. They stood together at the foot of the bed while Campbell tried coaxing the baby into breathing. It didn't respond.

"Slap its butt," Sayen hissed.

Campbell shook his head. "We don't do that anymore. That was covered in one of the many classes you missed."

"Fine, Mister Adorkable, do something!"

On her own, the baby balled her tiny fingers into fists and let out a cry that let the whole room know she was a fighter.

Relief swept through Campbell. He held that tiny bundle of bawling life in his hands as he gazed into Sayen's fatally blue eyes, and he felt something pass between them, something so warm and natural it felt, well... loving. There was no other word for it. Caught in the wonder of seeing new life emerge into the universe, so frail and so dependent on him, he felt his infatuation for Sayen blossom into something deeper, some unknown force he could only call love.

They worked as a team. Sayen took the baby to the waiting bath water while Campbell tended to the mother. Campbell glanced up to see Sayen fastidiously washing the tiny, pink body. Campbell saw warmth pour from Sayen as he fawned over the infant. It seemed as if their two bodies became one glowing force of nature, bound by some invisible strength. But even caught in that cocoon of heartfelt feelings, Sayen seemed to pull back.

Campbell moved to Sayen's side.

"I can't believe people are so hot to be strapped down with one of these," Sayen said. "I mean, they cry, keep you up all night, cost a fortune, and they smell."

The baby continued to cry as Campbell wrapped it in a blanket and handed her to Sayen. Nuzzling into Sayen's protective embrace, she stopped crying. Sayen pressed his cheek to the baby's forehead, humming a soothing tune.

Campbell nodded. "They give you unconditional love, which is something in short supply."

The baby seemed to smile. Both men shared a wonder-filled moment, drawn close to each other, with the baby between them. They could almost kiss.

Sayen broke away from the moment to cross the room and press the baby into its mother's arms. Mrs. Bishop's tears were now joyful. She cuddled her infant, then grabbed Sayen's hand and pulled him toward her like a fish on a line. She kissed his cheek, and a line of red moved up from Sayen's collar to cover his entire face.

Mrs. Bishop grabbed her husband and kissed him. "It's a girl. Honey, we have a baby girl. I love you. I love you so much."

Campbell crossed the room and slid an arm across Sayen's shoulders. "Look at them," Campbell whispered. "They're glowing. You think they care if it smells? That's why God made talcum powder."

"Okay, babies are adorable. I'll give you that. But for me, kids are like snow."

"Snow?"

"It's great when it belongs to someone else. You drive to it, play in it, and then drive home to your warm, dry house."

"It snows in Tripoli?"

"Are all Americans so stupid when it comes to world geography?"

Nurse Peggy rushed through the doorway. Dr. Crill strolled in behind her.

"Alright," Crill said, "are we ready to begin?"

CHAPTER TWO

CAMPBELL'S apartment was near campus, and the two men enjoyed a pleasant stroll there from the sushi restaurant. The rooms were spacious and cluttered with modern furnishings and artwork, and had large picture windows in the living room that allowed the evening light to drizzle in from a lavender sky.

Campbell led Sayen into the kitchen and selected a bottle of wine from a shelf above the counter.

Sayen took in the room with a slow careful glance, running his hand along the granite countertops, noting the stainless-steel pots and pans hanging from a rack over the island, visibly admiring the professional stove and two ovens. "You should have told me you had such a well-stocked kitchen. I could have cooked and saved you forty-five bucks."

"You cook?"

"I do a lamb curry from scratch that will singe the hair off your balls."

"You're making a pretty big assumption."

"That you have balls?"

"No, smartass, hair on them. I'm smooth as a baby down there."

Sayen selected two wineglasses from a cabinet while Campbell pulled the cork and poured. When he set the bottle down, Sayen took a quick peek at the label. "'95 Château Margaux Premier

Grand Cru Classé? Never heard of it. Of course, being a Muslim, I seldom drink alcohol, so I'm no connoisseur of fine wines."

Campbell handed Sayen a glass, and they meandered to the doorway with Campbell following. He noticed how Sayen's faded jeans hung loosely about that deceptively slim waist, giving a fashionable charm, discreetly suggesting the curve of that perfectly molded ass without going so far as to flaunt it. He admired Sayen's fitness, his strength. He had a body normally sculpted by a private athletics coach at a professional gym, but with Sayen, it was a natural work of art. It had to be, because Campbell knew Sayen didn't have the money for an athletic supporter, let alone an athletics coach. Watching this man's poise as he sauntered across the room inflamed a sudden passion in Campbell's chest. *He is curiously attractive, but not affected by it*, Campbell thought. *He doesn't flaunt his sex appeal, but rather, expects you to realize his greater, inner beauty.*

"You should have trained to be a chef, or maybe studied law. I mean, anything but medicine."

"I'll make a fine doctor," Sayen said. "Just not a surgeon. Pediatricians make tons of money and never see a drop of blood."

"And what about your plans to join Doctors Without Borders and go back to Libya to help your people? You think you won't see blood with a revolution brewing?"

"They're my people. I'll deal."

At the doorway to the living room, Campbell grabbed Sayen's arm and turned him around. Hastily, clumsily, as if jerking awake from a dreamless sleep, Campbell slipped his arm around Sayen's waist and hooked his fingers into a belt loop of Sayen's jeans and then leaned in for a kiss.

Sayen, turned his head away, unhooked Campbell's fingers from his belt loop, and pushed him back with a determined, but not unsympathetic smile.

That sudden and powerful passion that Campbell felt grew even stronger. He felt the heat of it burning his face, like acid dripping on every nerve ending.

"We had dinner because you saved my ass today," Sayen said, "but that's it."

They touched rims, all the while Campbell wondering what type of man Sayen was anyway. He seemed like such a delightful, yet enigmatic puzzle. "Here's to the end of virginity."

"Speak for yourself." Sayen sipped his wine, and his top lip moved over the fullness of the bottom one. His eyebrows rose at the quality, something he was clearly not used to. "Wow, this is sick."

Campbell stared into his eyes. "Are you talkin' about the wine or me?"

Sayen chuckled. "I'll be in the living room. Why don't you bring the bottle in case we need more?" He slipped through the doorway.

Campbell stared after him. *Need more? What I need is for you to hold me all through the night and not let me go. Never let me go.* The words echoing in his mind sounded like some hollow love song or a cliché message on a Hallmark card. The thought turned sour. He shook the notion from his head and turned his thoughts on the moment, of how comforting it felt to have Sayen here at his apartment, sharing a bottle of red. And who knew what else? He expected nothing on this first date, and yet, he was young enough that he expected everything on this first date too. *Yes,* he told himself, *enjoy the moment and be prepared for anything.*

Campbell took a deep, Adam's-apple-bobbing swallow of wine, and it tasted like courage. He pulled his inhaler from his pocket, gave himself a blast, and plowed into the living room. He found Sayen sprawled on the couch with the relaxed sleekness of a big game cat sleeping under a shade tree. Campbell ambled to the tuner and flipped on some music, easing the volume nob down several notches. He turned off one of the room lamps on his way to the couch, and settled well within Sayen's gravitational pull. He wanted so desperately to lean into this man, to lift that pout into a smile with a kiss. *What is it,* he thought, *that makes a pouting face so damned sexy?*

"Tell me more about this mysterious boyfriend," Campbell said.

"We're back on that subject? How boring."

"So bore me, I don't mind. What's the attraction?"

Sayen took a long swallow of wine. "He's a decent guy who helps me make ends meet."

"You're a kept boy?"

"Look, Cam, my middle name is Levon for a reason. I was named after that Elton John song because I was literally born a pauper, to a pawn, on Christmas Day."

"I love it when you call me Cam. My little sister is the only one who ever calls me that."

"You know, it's all so easy for you rich guys. You don't have a clue."

"I'm not rich, my parents are."

The sound system switched songs. The soft warble of Shane Mack singing "Lie to Me" floated on the air. Campbell shifted, trying to find a more comfortable position, and not finding one.

"Right," Sayen said, "you're one of those lucky trust-fund fucks who uses daddy's money to get whatever you want. You just point and take. But I've worked my ass raw to get to a position where I'm set. A few more years of grubbing, and I'll be one of those takers. Until then, I'm not rocking the boat."

Campbell picked up a remote control and notched down the lighting to a romantic glow. "Not rocking the boat? Hom, dating a married man is like standing in a leaking rowboat, for God sakes. I'm offering you the *QE2*."

"Modesty so becomes you."

"Are you this hard on everyone who falls in love with you?"

"Love?" Now it was Sayen's turn to shift around, looking for a more comfortable spot. Campbell leaned closer, giving no route to escape. Sayen looked away, his expression complicated, unreadable.

"Don't tell me you haven't noticed," Campbell said.

Sayen took another deep swallow of wine. "I don't even know what love means, and neither do you. You see something you want and you take. Well, guess what, I'm not a something."

"I do know about love." Campbell grinned while pouring more wine into Sayen's glass. "You go all out for what you want, you don't let a lack of money stop you from your dream, and you're the kind of man who joins DWB and learns to deal with your phobia about blood in order to help your people." He looked up from filling his own glass. "You're special, and that intrigues me. Everything about you intrigues me. Isn't that important?"

Sayen cleared his throat. "Before my mother died, I promised her I would become someone respectable, someone everybody looked up to. Right now, for me at least, that's all that's important." Sayen pulled a white monogrammed handkerchief from his pocket. It unfolded and hung between them.

Campbell smiled. "You're surrendering?"

"This is yours, remember?"

Campbell pushed it back. "Consider it the first of many presents I'll lavish on you."

"Wow, Mr. Big Spender gives me a handkerchief. I'm so impressed."

"You should be. You see that monogram? My mother hand-stitched that. It's the only thing she ever made for me, and she only made two. So you see, I'm giving you something I cherish."

Sayen pressed the cloth to his cheek. "Wow, I am impressed. But what would you tell your lily-white, Catholic parents? They'll think I'm a terrorist."

Sayen's question somehow sounded like a capitulation. Campbell felt something reckless well up inside him; a sense of euphoria filled him to overflowing. He set down his wine, inched closer, and slid one arm over Sayen's shoulder. "I'm going to help you fulfill that promise you made to your mother, even if it hair-lips the Pope. Here's the plan." He unbuttoned the top button of Sayen's shirt. "Step one: admit that you would rather be with me than some old married dude who's afraid to be seen with you." Campbell briefly kissed Sayen's shoulder while Sayen closed his eyes and spun the wine in his glass round and round as if he were turning a prayer wheel.

Campbell unbuttoned the next button and found a patch of silky hair covering hard muscle. The fine hair curled around his fingers as if with joy for having been discovered. His head began to tingle at that feathery touch. "Step two: you move in with me."

Sayen's eyes pinched more firmly shut; the soft pink of his lips nearly disappeared. Campbell kissed Sayen's neck, and unclasped the next button. "Three, take your boyfriend to your favorite restaurant and tell him you will always be grateful to him, but I'm taking care of you now." He kissed Sayen's cheek as he brushed his hand through that glorious forest of chest hair. He undid the last button. "Then you let my charm and Daddy's money make your promise come true."

He kissed Sayen's lips, longer, fervently. He spread Sayen's shirt open, ran his hand down Sayen's chest. After years of cautious glances and hopeful yearning—on the basketball court, in the gym locker room and showers, even watching Sayen at the library losing himself in a book—he could now barely contain himself. Though he'd had sex with other men, touching had never felt like this. The fullness in Sayen's shoulders and chest was chiseled without seeming bulky. The texture was supple skin over granite muscle, and that hair, that splendid fur curving into a thin, dark line that journeyed down the middle of his rippled stomach and widened again below his navel. Having seen Sayen in the gym showers, Campbell knew he shaved his underarms as well as his pubic hair, apparently a custom in some Muslim cultures, but thank God he didn't shave his chest, arms, and legs.

Campbell rolled an erect nipple between thumb and forefinger. He edged closer until he felt an unbearable fire spread over his own chest and groin, extending into a faint wash of heat through his head. He could smell the fruit of wine on Sayen's spent breath, feel the muscles tightening at his touch. That skin, that supple, bronzed softness seemed to burn his fingertips. He pulled back to admire the treasure trail leading below.

Does he really want me, or only Daddy's money? What the hell am I doing? I will never be worthy of him; he is too fine, too good-looking, too pure. He will never be interested in me. No, damn it, sit up straight, look sexy, be confident. I can do this.

Sayen opened his eyes, and a faint light seemed to shine from within their depths. That piercing look froze all Campbell's thoughts. It was the same look Sayen had shown when they had held that baby between them, caught in the wonder of new life. But then those eyes, blue as sapphires, seemed to slide away, to look across the room. Searching for an escape route?

Campbell read something in the sudden change in mood. Fear? Guilt? An anguished indecision? Or was Sayen's wary caution morphing into something like mourning?

Campbell shivered in the instant he lost all his confidence. He knew he had done something wrong, pushed too fast, too hard. He had somehow caused this beautiful man to feel pain.

"I'm sorry," Sayen said. "All this is new to me. I've only had two lovers. The first was my brother, Mahmud. He was twenty then, five years older than me. We slept in the same bed. One night he came home after he had been drinking with his chums. He was crazy with lust. He pulled my pajamas down and fucked me, and because he was my older brother, I had to submit. In my culture it's not that uncommon. He's not gay; he just needed to get off, and I was available. When that began to happen regularly, my mother brought me to the United States to protect me from Mahmud's lust. She said it was to keep me from the growing violence against our family, but I know the real reason. What neither of them knew was how deeply I loved him, before and after he raped me."

Campbell sat shocked and embarrassed. What he felt about any type of incest was unadulterated revulsion. To hide his own prejudices, he tried to move the conversation to safer ground. "And the second one is this married sugar daddy?"

"After my mother died, I couldn't go back to Tripoli because by then I knew I was gay, and life for a gay Muslim in North Africa is no picnic. I needed someone to help me survive here, and he has. Before I met him, I was adept at dining on fumes."

"Fumes?"

"I'd sit at a table nursing a coffee or latte, and absorb the delectable fragrances of the meals being served all around me. I could make a single latte last a whole evening."

Campbell pressed his face to that beautifully formed neck and lingered below the jawline until the pleasure grew unbearable. His lips brushed Sayen's satiny mouth before pulling away.

The room grew intensely quiet despite the soft music.

Campbell fingered Sayen's shirt, pulling it further open to reveal more flesh. "We've run out of buttons," Campbell said to ease his sudden discomfiture.

A smile graced Sayen's face, and in the dim light he looked like a lost angel, luminous and acquiescent. He breathed faster, harder, and stammered, "There's one more."

Even before Campbell's mind reengaged to understand what those three little words meant, his fingers had already reached for the button on Sayen's jeans. This time Sayen kissed Campbell, forcefully moving his tongue into Campbell's mouth as if laying claim to new territory. A devouring, breathless kiss. Sayen pulled away. "You really love me?"

Campbell saw a plea in those alluring eyes; it drew him closer. Those eyes were begging, but then they glazed over while moisture collected in the corners, until a single drop formed, trapped in those lashes until he blinked. The drop slid down his cheek, and he brushed it away with the back of his hand.

Campbell popped that last button open.

CHAPTER THREE

A WIND rose to a keening whine. Lilies and a bowl of oranges adorned a gravestone on which the name Sue-Jin Hommet, two dates, and the words NOT FORGOTTEN were carved.

Sayen Hommet crouched on his knees over his prayer rug before the gravestone. He lit three incense sticks and placed them in a marble holder, bobbing up and down three times like a bird doing a mating dance. He went utterly still, staring into space in a Zen-like trance. His focus lifted slightly higher than the line of trees at the edge of the road, and he watched the smooth flight of a line of pelicans. He studied their sleek contours like da Vinci would have done, and that pulled him into a deeper state of concentration.

Kneeling amid rows of headstones on a Thursday afternoon, gazing at nothing in particular, as if staring through a window into another dimension, he opened himself up to all that is, offering himself to the loving energy that binds the universe, until he felt himself become weightless, floating.

Any bystanders would have presumed he was steeped in prayer, but Sayen believed in stopping all conscious thought, to open his mind to Allah and merge with the life force of the cosmos so it would send him a message or move him in the right direction. And just then, what he hoped for most was a sign—move forward or retreat.

He had only spent a few days with Campbell, but already it felt like he had stepped beyond the looking glass into a fantasy. He didn't love Campbell, but he did love what Campbell could do for him, and the fact that Campbell was attentive and adorable only added to Sayen's delight. But could it last? Would Campbell tire of footing the bill? Should Sayen give up a sure bet on this capricious long shot? He felt like a surfer balanced on the arch of a wave, caught between two worlds, trying to snatch a few perilous minutes of bliss before the wall of water came crashing over his head. The larger part of him screamed to stay with the sure bet, but then the binding threads of his fear uncoiled, and he remembered that first night with Campbell, of drowning in golden kisses, like sunlight splaying into a warm sea while he sank deeper and deeper. Their lovemaking had grown rougher; stroking, nibbling, biting. He now pictured them wrestling for dominance on the living room rug, heard the soft gasps of wonder as they twisted and rolled, groping with fingers and mouths, caresses turning into smacks. He had expected his passion to level off, but the rising intensity pushed them both further and further as their lovemaking became an assault. It felt primal, and he had been swept away in it. They had broken apart for what seemed an instant as Campbell ran to the bedroom to retrieve his lube and condoms. The battle for dominance continued until Campbell surrendered and accepted Sayen's erection into his body. With an overpowering sense of supremacy, Sayen had fucked him hard, unrelenting. Cocooned in that wild ferocity, Sayen had felt his veneer fall away until he became utterly innocent and genuine for the first time with another man. That feeling had left him with a sense of astonishment, like riding a horse over a sheer cliff.

He had not allowed Campbell to screw him, although Campbell had wanted to. Only one man had ever fucked Sayen, and right then Sayen pictured his brother's face hovering over his prone body, the thin mustache and those fervent, liquid eyes, and his copious prick standing proud and impatient as it pressed into Sayen's backside.

Crouched on the carpet, Sayen flexed his buttocks and parted his thighs as he remembered the feel of his brother's thrusts, and how Sayen had taken pleasure from his assaults. And he knew that it was out of love for his brother that he would not—would never—take that same pleasure from Campbell.

Sayen realized that his mind had wandered. His memories had made him hard and deepened his breathing. With effort, he cleared his mind and opened himself to Allah once more, hoping for a sign.

Thirty minutes spanned into an hour, then two. A light rain fell. The incense sticks had long burned out, but the wet breeze kept its steady pulse against this face. The wind pressed against him like a living force.

A piece of paper cartwheeled on the wind, slapping against the gravestone with a wet splat. It was an advertisement for a pool company. A corner of the paper folded over, revealing the bolded words: "Take The Plunge!"

Sayen flashed a grateful smile. He reached for the paper, but it flew away.

"Thank you, Mother," he whispered.

He hiked his scarf tighter around his neck and bowed three times while mumbling prayers. He rolled up his prayer rug, hurried toward his rescued Mini Cooper—another of Campbell's gifts—and piled in. He peered out the driver's window at his mother's grave as the car pulled away. His Mona Lisa smile reflected back at him in the glass.

CHAPTER FOUR

CHANDELIERS sparkled like diamonds. The Mark Hopkins Hotel dining room was a place where some came to flaunt, and others came to dream. Sayen strolled into the waiting area and clasped hands with Andre (whose real name was Fred) the maître d'.

"He's at your favorite table," Andre said.

"How long has he been waiting?"

Andre smiled. "Two Scotches."

"Shit. Have Bernard bring my usual."

As Sayen floated across the room, he sized up Blake sitting at a table for two. He sported a tussore-silk suit of superlative cut, and a Panama hat tilted so the brim hid his right eye. Blake's impeccable grooming reflected the high value he placed on appearances, and the hat that partially hid his face broadcasted his need for secrecy. *What a shame to hide his head*, Sayen thought. Strangely enough, it was Blake's salt-and-pepper hair, growing snowy white at the temples, that made him most attractive in Sayen's eyes. There was something about an older man, that power and respectability one acquires with age that drew Sayen like the moon draws water. He watched Blake knock back his drink while impatiently twirling a small gift-wrapped box.

As Sayen slid into the seat across from Blake, the older man snatched the gift-wrapped box under the table.

"Sorry I'm late," Sayen said. "What are you hiding?"

"It's nothing. What kept you this time?"

Bernard minced up and set a cup of sweetened tea on the table. Blake lifted his glass, indicating another Glenlivet.

Sayen sipped his drink while gazing out the window at the city skyline. He leaned closer to Blake and inhaled the way he remembered his mother sniffing a rose. He was rewarded with the rich compound of whisky, aftershave lotion, and shoe polish. Under all that he detected the faint rankness of mature male. He loved that smell, but tonight it made him sad. "What a lovely sunset. I wouldn't mind the nights if they were colorful. The blackness feels claustrophobic, like the inside of a coffin."

"And I wouldn't mind if you paid more attention to me."

Sayen swiveled his head toward Blake, flashing a sudden smile. "Sorry. I visited my mother's grave today, and I was thinking of a vow I made her. Sounds like someone had a tense day?"

"On a scale of one to ten, I'll be showing up on the chart any minute."

Sayen slipped his foot from his shoe and rubbed it against Blake's calf. Blake sneaked sideways looks at the other diners to ensure nobody noticed. Sayen's foot rode up Blake's leg, along his thigh, and nuzzled in the older man's crotch. Blake pressed his legs together, squeezing the foot, refusing to let go. Sayen watched a blush smolder from Blake's white collar to his hairline.

"On the chart yet?" Sayen crooned, as his toes gently played in Blake's crotch.

Blake signaled the waiter. "Let's eat and get the hell out of here."

"Someone's in a hurry for dessert?"

Bernard delivered two menus, but neither Sayen nor Blake took one. "We're pressed for time tonight, Bernard," Sayen said.

"Naturally," Bernard said, with a tip of his head.

"We'll both have the Caesar salad," Sayen said, "rare ahi tuna steaks, and the '95 Château Margaux Cru Classé."

Bernard's eyebrows rose at the mention of the wine, and his lips lifted into a grin. Sayen assumed the waiter was already calculating his tip on a five-hundred-dollar bottle of wine.

As Bernard shuffled away, Sayen turned to Blake half expecting a protest but knowing the man would not embarrass himself by overriding the order. "Happy? I wanted tonight to be special. We're going all out."

"That's perfect," Blake said. "Special is good. I didn't know you had such good taste. When did you begin learning about wines?"

"I'm taking a crash course on style. It's so exhausting I can barely drag myself out of bed."

"I have a few surprises of my own." Blake placed the gift-wrapped box on the table and slid it toward Sayen.

Without showing much interest, Sayen unwrapped the box and removed a diamond-studded Omega watch.

"You've admired mine so often," Blake said, "I thought you would like one."

"Let me see yours."

Blake hesitated, then removed his watch and passed it to Sayen.

The younger man compared the identical watches, noting that Blake's watch had an inscription on the back from his wife. He read the message and smiled, then handed the new watch back to Blake.

"You can't have mine," Blake said.

"I don't want something you buy me. I want something you cherish." Sayen saw the confusion in the older man's eyes, and he began to feel sorry for him, for them both.

Blake hesitated for a few more moments, then spread his legs, releasing Sayen's foot. Sayen reluctantly slid his foot back into his shoe.

"I don't see why we couldn't eat in the room," Blake said.

"I thought an elegant dinner and conversation would make our rendezvous more memorable."

It was true. He wanted to remember this night, this fine moment with Blake for the rest of his life. He could feel the sadness growing in his gut, and he forced himself to focus exclusively on the man across the table. They still had a few precious hours to enjoy themselves.

Blake cleared his throat. "After two years you finally want more? I mean, that's wonderful, because I want more too. I do. But you know I don't appreciate you bringing me here."

Not again, Sayen thought with a sigh. *He bitches every time I drag him here, even though he enjoys every minute of it.* "What, the waiters aren't cute enough?"

"You know I hate being seen in public."

Yes, and that is the problem, isn't it, Sayen thought as Bernard sauntered up to present the wine. Sayen glanced at the label and nodded. They were both silent as Bernard uncorked the bottle and poured a splash into Sayen's glass. Sayen noted the color, which reminded him of currants and black olives. He sniffed. He had read this wine has a complex nose, but he had no idea what that meant. He sipped and felt a warm, full-bodied sensation trickle down his throat, making all his taste buds stand up and salute. *This wine is like Blake,* he thought; *it is like buried treasure that you have to search for, and it's there.* "Fabulous," he said to Bernard. He turned to Blake. "I read this wine will be best after 2014, but I can't wait."

As soon as Bernard had poured two glasses and sauntered away, Blake said, "I'm sorry, but you know I can't be seen by certain people."

"We're back on that subject? Look, all these men are doing the same thing we are. Once, for grins, I shouted 'Dad, what are you doing here?' I swear, every geezer in the room dropped his dentures in his lap."

Clearly not amused, Blake scanned the room. Nearly every table had an older gentleman sitting with a much younger lady or even younger man. Blake turned back to Sayen. "My point is: somebody here might know me. I want to see more of you, but not in public."

"First you pout because I want us to enjoy a memorable dinner, now you want to see more of me?" Sayen lifted his glass. "Here's to the one place we are perfectly safe to be seen together. Now drink your wine."

They touched rims and Blake tasted the wine. His eyes grew large. "This is superlative. You really are the best, and you bring what's best to me. I'm grateful."

Sayen felt a flush of bittersweet joy.

"In fact, I'm so grateful," Blake continued, "that I want you to live in the city, so I can pop in more often. I'll buy you a condo, pay the bills, give you an allowance. You'll be set."

Rather than take another sip of Château Margaux, Sayen stared into Blake's large, hopeful eyes. "Did we just tumble into the twilight zone? If you want that kind of a relationship, you can start by telling me your real name, Mr. Smith…."

The shock on Blake's face would have been noticeable from across the room. His voice grew to a shout. "Dammit, I'm in love with you."

Conversations halted; people stared.

"I want to take care of you," Blake said in a much softer voice.

"You want to own me!"

Bernard wheeled a cart to the table. Sayen saw amusement ruffling through him.

"Sorry to interrupt," Bernard said, "but you did say you were pressed for time."

Sayen and Blake glared at each other while Bernard prepared and served the salad. Blake lifted his wineglass and sipped. As Bernard glided away, Blake said, "I'm offering you a chance to finish school with no financial worries."

Sayen still felt the heat of anger. "So how is that different than our current arrangement, I mean, other than I'd be at your beck and call?"

Blake bit his lip in an obvious attempt to hold his temper. "I'm making you a generous offer."

Sayen saw resentment pull Blake's skin taut over his forehead, smoothing out those distinguished wrinkles, making the older man look as vulgar as an aggressive pit bull terrier. But Sayen was suddenly beyond caring. "Generous? You want to lock me away and have me when nobody's looking. You're too gutless to give me something so obvious as matching rings, so you give me this fucking watch. That's your grand idea of love?"

The wineglass in Blake's hand shattered. Wine sprayed across the table. Shards of glass punctured Blake's palm.

Sayen jumped to the older man's side, rangy as a greyhound, pulsating with regret and apprehension. He took that injured hand and expertly removed the shards. The sight of blood had his head spinning, and for a moment he thought he might pass out cold, but he focused on the task and pushed himself beyond his phobia. He also had to restrain himself from hugging Blake, to comfort the older man and to ease his own sudden shame.

Bernard came running, looking ready to faint at the sight of that bloody hand.

"Bernard," Sayen hissed, "bring me a first-aid kit and a martini."

"I'm bleeding to death and all you can think of is a drink?"

"Oh, that is so not right."

Bernard rushed up with both drink and kit, and sat them on the table. As Sayen removed the last bit of glass, he patted away the blood with his napkin, then lifted the martini and poured the alcohol over the wounds. He ripped open the kit and efficiently bandaged the hand while Bernard cleaned up the table as best he could.

Blake, looking suddenly sheepish, said, "Nice to know those medical courses I'm paying for are being put to good use."

Sayen avoided looking into the older man's eyes as he tied the bandage and sat in his chair. He wanted so desperately to give the man something heartfelt, but the evening had taken a bad turn and there seemed little point in trying to salvage it now.

Blake examined his bandaged hand. He also seemed to be searching for a way to rescue the evening.

"You're right," Sayen finally said, not able to stand the silence any longer. "It's a very generous offer, and I'm grateful. It's just that I've got another deal cooking, so I'll have to turn you down."

Bernard brought a fresh wineglass to the table, but Blake waved him away.

"Another deal? What the hell does that mean?"

Sayen took a deep breath to buck up his courage. "I'd planned to tell you in the room, afterwards, that a dream lover has fallen for me. This is our last date." There, he had said it, and from the pain rising on Blake's face, he knew that he had burned that bridge to ash. Things would never be the same; there was no going back now.

Blake turned away, staring out the window. His voice went soft. "Do you love him?"

Sayen felt a sudden stab in his chest, but he would not allow himself to back down now. "He gives me more than a condo. He gives me class. I can finally live openly with someone who is proud to be seen with me. He makes me feel, you know, respectable.... And he's loaded."

Blake smiled. The smile looked genuine enough. The look of awe warmed into something human, sympathetic, as Blake gave a slight jerk of his head that might have stood for a wry laugh. "Does he know how you make your money?"

Sayen felt his back stiffen, and for a moment his self-restraint seemed to stick in his throat, making his words sound funny. "Like you tell your wife everything? Please understand, I've been on my knees panning for nuggets since my mom died. I've finally hit the mother lode, and nothing will stop me now...."

Sayen sipped his wine carefully, letting that full-bodied flavor fill the emptiness in his chest. He could feel the moment, like this relationship, squeezing shut like a beautiful flower at its peak being plucked and pressed into the pages of a thick book. He felt the soft petals crumple as the pages pushed together, crushing, parching the life out of it. He felt that many years from now, he would turn the pages of his life back and look at this pressed moment, preserved and remembered, dry and flat, the color faded. That once beautiful flower would be brittle and perfectly dead.

CHAPTER FIVE

HALLE had already walked a longer distance than she had in months, but she considered that a bonus, because her doctor had lectured her about expectant mothers needing exercise. She passed a counter displaying a hundred different shades of Maybelline lipsticks manned by a smiling, obviously gay, Macy's sales clerk. Beyond the clerk she saw her reflection in a mirror that covered the wall. Her black dress and boots, heavy gothic makeup, and piercings didn't fit this light, airy environment. She stood out like a circus freak at a church social.

She felt deeply tired, but she pushed her weariness and sore back from her thoughts, as well as her swollen belly. She also ignored all the staring people, the colorful displays, and the excited shouts of children. Her focal point zeroed in on the man at her side, Rachid. He was a few years into adulthood, a month shy of twenty-two, and four years older than she. He was a perfect physical specimen. Every part of him was athletic and firm, with rich brown skin and a goatee that accented his perfect teeth on those rare times he smiled. He resembled a young Rudolph Valentino, and she adored his beauty, but just then he showed the charmless arrogance in his gaze that reminded her of a spirited racehorse that submits patiently to being petted. They strolled arm in arm, leisurely, needing nothing more than to be with each other.

"You know," Rachid said, "if Macy's had a no-gay hiring policy, this store would be completely self-serve."

Halle winced. "You don't have to put other people down just to build yourself up. I think you're fine the way you are."

"Hey, I'm not putting those mutants down. I'm just saying."

"No, you're doing much more than saying. You're showing what a condescending ass you can be."

She felt his hand tighten on hers, not quite to the point of being painful.

"That is no way to talk to your future husband. In my culture, women must show respect for their men, especially in public."

"Yes," Halle said, "in Islam women have no rights, only duties." Now his hand squeezed harder, and it did hurt. She knew he had only been trying to amuse her, but she hated that side of him. She understood even more than he did how her words, first against him and then against Islam, could bruise his ego. She felt dangerously light-headed. "I'm sorry," she whispered while bowing her head, knowing full well that what had been said cannot be unsaid or forgotten. This was the reality of relationships. Who should know better than she after being his lover for the last ten months?

"As well you should be," he said in an overly loud voice while jerking away from her. His elbow connected with a crystal ten-inch-high floral arrangement on the counter, knocking it to the floor. It made a shocking noise as it hit the floor. Halle sensed all eyes turning toward her. Shards of glass littered the white tiles.

For a moment, everything seemed to go quiet except for the intercom softly playing crematorium music. Without thinking, she bent to pick up the fake flowers, but he pulled her back. The air hung heavy with the scents of several perfumes, all mingling, making Halle feel slightly nauseous. She glanced up to see a headless mannequin wearing a snow-white wedding dress that glittered, which had the surprising effect of making her even more nauseated.

Rachid wrapped his arm around her shoulder and escorted her away from all those staring eyes. As they hurried toward the baby section, she couldn't get the sight of that headless mannequin out of her mind.

He led her to a table of baby clothes, and they both browsed the colorful patterns.

"When a wife loves her husband, then respect for her man is her expression of love, rather than a duty," he said, resuming their conversation. "You must see it in the right light."

"The love I dream about," she said, realizing for the first time that her love for him didn't measure up to her standard, was feeble by comparison, "is a love that I choose to spend my life with a man, every minute, not because of some marriage vow or some religious custom or because that's what society expects, but because there is no other person I would rather devote my life to."

He wrapped his arm around her waist and squeezed hard, as if to shut her up rather than a show of affection.

"I want my future husband to know that what I give is pure, and I expect that same feeling back from him. It has to go both ways, equal."

She looked into his face for a response, but he remained silent. His eyes dropped to the baby clothes, and he held up a blue jumper, admiring it.

She knew he didn't agree, but she continued, "Love must be a living, tangible thing, even if we are from different cultures. I don't want to marry anyone if I don't feel that unbelievable magic that I know is possible." She moved her hands, one to her heart and the other to her swollen belly. "When two people surrender completely to each other, they become a whole, complete entity. Think about that. Half of yourself will never enslave the other half."

He sighed. "This kind of love does not come quickly. You will marry me, and care for our son, and in time you will learn to love me in this way."

"Rachid, you're so clueless." She turned and made a beeline for the exit doors. He caught up to her and clasped his hand on her arm, squeezing tight, but she kept walking.

"Halle, I get it, but you're talking about a dream. I'm talking about real life, our future."

They were both quiet for the time it took to reach the exit and pass through the glass doors leading to the sidewalk. She was certain she should let the conversation die, let him think he had won, had beaten her into submission once again, but she had grown tired of that response to his mental bullying.

The sidewalk had a stream of shoppers hurrying by. The street was choked with traffic; the exhaust fumes seemed overpowering, and the blare from horns stretched Halle's nerves tighter than violin strings. As she joined the flow of pedestrians, Rachid fell in step beside her.

"What I said, if you had paid any attention, is that I have no intention of marrying you. My love for you is not pure, and I'm not going to marry you just to give my baby your name."

He grabbed her by both arms and shook her hard enough to rattle teeth. "You will be my wife! I will not have a bastard child raised by a whore."

The crowd of shoppers parted around them like the parting of the Red Sea. Nobody came to her aid. Nobody cared. They simply stared at the spectacle she had become.

"I'm a whore because you made me one. And I have no intention of raising your child. My mother has arranged to have it adopted by a Christian family."

He released her, dropped his arm to his side, and stepped back. Shock was palpable in his eyes. Halle felt immediately sorry she had let that particular cat out of the bag, but now that it was out, there was nothing to do but deal with it. Her stomach began to move. She felt a solid kick, and another. It seemed there was someone else who protested the idea of being raised a Christian.

"You mean to kill me, is that it?" he spat.

"Don't be such a drama queen."

He balled up a right fist and smashed his left palm. "If you have any feelings for me at all, you must not do this. You will marry me, and we will raise our child within the true religion."

"Rachid, I'm a minor. You've heard of statutory rape? If my parents find out you're the father, they'll have you thrown in prison. Get it?"

"My child must be raised a Muslim, even if you refuse to marry me."

"I won't make any promises. The only thing I know is that we can't marry, not because of the law, but because we don't love each other like that." She felt another solid kick to her ribs.

"We will in time," Rachid said, with a pleading tone.

She knew it was a lie, and from the tenor of his voice, she could tell he also knew. She turned and walked away, jostling through all the oncoming pedestrians. As she fought her way to the end of the block with tears sliding down her cheeks, she pulled out her cell phone and called the one man she did love heart and soul.

CHAPTER SIX

CAMPBELL'S back pressed into the leather seat of his Porsche 911 as he braced himself for another curve. His lead foot didn't ease up as the car hugged the Coast Highway asphalt. The car's top was down; wind riffled through his sweat-dampened hair. With the ocean so near, he could smell vaporized salt and seaweed with every intoxicating breath. It was a scent that epitomized the freedom of late summer, but Campbell felt his stomach slowly turning. Not from the smell or from the car's speed, but from what lay ahead. He tried focusing instead on sharing the cockpit with Sayen and letting the smell of the sea fill his choked lungs, but that quiet trepidation kept creeping back into his thoughts.

"I feel sick," Campbell said. "Is this really wise?"

Sayen held a white-knuckle grip on the door handle. "You mean driving like Mario Andretti on amphetamines?"

Campbell braked as he sped into another curve. "I can drop you downtown. I'll have the birthday dinner with my folks, and we'll hookup after. We'll have a drink, then dash to the airport."

"Who are you ashamed of, them or me?"

Campbell scowled at Sayen. How could he be ashamed of this man who had already become the center of his world? He'd never met anyone before with whom spending time was more comfortable than being alone. Other men were exciting, beautiful, entertaining, but never comfortable.

"Cam, don't worry," Sayen said. "And watch the road."

Campbell had taken his eyes off the road for a dangerously long time. When he faced forward again, he hit the brakes hard and slid sideways into a curve. He fought to control it and managed to right the car while slowing to a reasonable speed.

When they were both relatively calm again, Sayen wound the knob of the radio past random bursts of static until he stopped on Tina Turner singing "What's Love Got To Do With It."

"But what if they freak?" Campbell whined.

Sayen barked a sharp laugh. "Yes, they'll discover that the sparkle of their eye, straight-A student, and nothing to confess on Sundays, takes it up the bum."

Surprise caught Campbell in his throat, closing his windpipe. His lungs labored and his eyes streamed as he fumbled in his pocket for his inhaler. One blast and he could almost relax. He even smiled.

In the back of the SUV ahead of them, three adolescent boys waged war among the boogie boards and wetsuits and beach balls. The battle turned from fighting each other to making faces and rude gestures at the Porsche. Sayen made faces back at them, egging the boys on.

Campbell's cell phone buzzed. He fished it out of his pocket. "Speak to me."

"It's baa baa black sheep," said a voice through the phone. "Can you pick me up downtown?"

"No problem," Campbell said. "ETA is fifteen minutes. Be out front of Macy's." Campbell dropped his phone in his pocket. "We're picking up my kid sister."

The Porsche sped into a residential area above Cliff House and stopped at a light on Geary Street. Two men in muscle shirts pushed a high-tech baby stroller across the intersection. They were both about Sayen's age, pumped up in their upper bodies but not their legs, and both looked bored and hot. They walked almost pressed together as if joined at the hip and were obviously a couple. Sayen waved at them, and they waved back, both smiling broadly.

Sayen leaned across the cockpit and kissed Campbell on the mouth.

Campbell jerked away. "Jesus, Hom. Not in public."

"This is San Francisco, not Tripoli. Besides," he said, shrugging good-humoredly, "no one will see us. Gays are invisible the world over—didn't you know?"

Campbell pushed Sayen back, putting a foot of space between them. "It's easy for you because you have nothing to lose, but if my parents freak, there goes my tuition, my car, my allowance, everything. I'm screwed, we're screwed, end of story. We need to break this gently, and that means no public displays."

Sayen, visibly put off, pointed to the baby carriage. "Never thought they'd let gays adopt."

"And we should tell them we're just dating," Campbell said. "They don't need to know we're living together."

Sayen's jaw dropped. "You are ashamed of me. What the fuck! Just dump me at the side of the road like the rest of the trash. That way you won't have to lie about me, just about you."

"No, no! It's not you," Campbell whined. "I guess I'm ashamed of myself. No, that's not it either. Shit... I just don't like hurting people, and this is going to hurt."

"So I'm not people? It's okay to hurt me but not your folks?"

"Hom, I'm sorry. I didn't mean—"

Sayen grabbed the back of Campbell's neck and gently squeezed. "Cam, give them some credit. Give me some too. I'll charm their socks off. Trust me, okay?"

Campbell stomped on the gas, and they accelerated through the intersection.

SAYEN remained silent for the drive into downtown. He had never had a boyfriend who wanted to show him off to his family before now, and he couldn't help feeling nervous. He wanted to make a great first impression, but more importantly, he wanted to fit into this affluent lifestyle as if he'd been born sucking on a silver spoon. As they crested one of San Francisco's seven hills and sped down into a forest of high-rises reaching into the dome of azure sky, Sayen

felt a drop of sweat slide from under his arm, down his flank.
Another drop made the same journey on his other side.

He held a tight grip on the door handle as the Porsche squealed
through an intersection and pulled to the curb in front of Macy's
department store. A few yards away, he saw a sullen, seven-month
pregnant teenager in gothic drag impatiently spinning a shopping
bag.

Sayen felt his jaw go slack and his mouth drop open as the
girl, who he now assumed was Halle Reardon, advanced to the car.
She and Campbell could not be more different.

As she came near, Campbell called to her. "I hope you got him
something dignified." In a softer voice he told Sayen that last year
she had given her father a cockring and a pair of handcuffs.

Halle's mouth curved into a full-lipped pout. She reached
under Sayen's chin and closed his mouth. "Omygod! Tell me
Golden Boy is not coming out to the folks on Dildo's birthday. That
is soooo harsh."

Sayen held his hand out to her. "I'm Sayen Hommet, the
boyfriend. But I gather you figured that out. Love your piercings."

She made no attempt to shake his hand, but rather, glared at
him as if he had made a vulgar remark.

"Just get in the car, sis," Campbell said. "And be civil."

"Bite me!"

Sayen opened the car door and slid onto the console, giving
her enough room to squeeze into the passenger seat. He draped one
arm over her shoulder and one over Campbell's. There was
something about her, something that fired a blaze of admiration in
his chest. She seemed a handful, and clearly wore her emotions on
her sleeve without a hint of pretention. He liked that, liked her. She
seemed much more real than her brother. The warmth of this little
family scene spread from his chest to his head, and he felt his lips
lifting into a comfortable grin.

As the Porsche roared away from the curb, she said, "Now that
you're coming out, maybe Dildo will stop spraying his shorts every
time some geek professor gives you an A. He'll probably even give
me the money I need for my boob job."

"Dildo?" Sayen asked.

Campbell shifted into a higher gear. "She means my father. She has issues because dad is more generous with me."

"More generous?" Halle barked. "*Hello*! Golden Boy walks on water, and I'm the pond scum between his toes."

Campbell laughed. "If you'd drop the Morticia Addams look and get off your ass in school, he'd be generous with you too."

Under his arm, Sayen could feel her stiffen, like a tigress preparing to leap.

"What, pretend I'm Mary Poppins like you?" she said. "Some of us can't hide our faults in the closet."

Sayen glanced down at her swollen belly and grinned wider. "There's nothing wrong with playing a part in order to reap the benefits. We all do it."

Her jaw locked into a stubborn line. "I want the world to accept me for the angry, insecure, confused bitch that I am and give me my due." She pointed an accusing finger at Campbell. "And you'll be singing a different tune once Dildo gets a look at your boy toy."

"One more boy toy slur and you're walking," Campbell snapped.

Sayen felt an overpowering desire to hug her. "Look on the bright side. I mean, look at you," he said. "You're creating life. You look so freakin' luminous. And no matter how your folks treat you, they can't take that beauty away from you. I'd trade places with you in a heartbeat."

She turned to stare into his eyes, and he saw her pupils glowing. No, it was not a trick of the sun; he clearly saw some spark of consuming life smoldering at her core. She was, in fact, luminous. She held his stare for only a moment, and turned away. Her face transformed into a mask that was at once radiant, yet achingly vulnerable.

"You're too much," she mumbled.

"You're welcome," Sayen said.

CHAPTER SEVEN

CAMPBELL'S Porsche zipped along the posh Sea Cliff neighborhood, pulled into a driveway, and stopped before an impressive iron gate. Behind stone walls that were high enough to ensure privacy, sprawled an acre of flawlessly-groomed landscaping surrounding an Italian-design villa nestled on a bluff overlooking a beach with a view of the Golden Gate Bridge. A rose garden beside the house provided splashes of yellow and magenta, and beyond that crouched a small waterfall shimmering into an iridescent swimming pool. What stood before Sayen was a dream, a vision he had held for many years but had never taken solid form before now. He was moments away from realizing that aspiration. His throat dried and his tongue swelled. He tried to swallow but couldn't. Sayen had known his lover's family was wealthy, but he had not expected this brazen level of opulence.

Campbell stamped a code into a keypad, and the gates yawned open. The car lunged forward and halted beside an antique Bentley. All three occupants piled out of the Porsche.

A squad of servants carried floral arrangements from a van into the house, and uniformed gardeners manicured the flowerbeds, but Sayen didn't notice. Drawn to the Bentley, he caressed the cream-colored, high-gloss paint as he peered inside at the immaculate leather seats and wood finishes. A long slow whistle escaped his lips.

He felt small and insignificant standing beside it. *The painstaking cleanness reflected the man who owned it,* he thought. *My new father-in-law. The car personified the man.*

"It's immaculate," Sayen said.

"If you don't keep it clean, you don't respect it," Campbell and Halle said at the same time, obviously mimicking their father's voice.

Halle laughed. "Dildo's pride and joy. Not even Golden Boy is allowed to touch it. In fact, it's the only thing Dildo loves more than Golden Boy." She grabbed Sayen's sleeve and towed him toward the house.

Sayen glanced back at the Bentley and then at the house and the perfectly groomed yard. Suddenly everything he saw seemed crucially important, chastising him for his previous poverty, mocking him. He swallowed the lump in his throat as he passed through the front double-door entrance.

Sayen followed Campbell and Halle through a spacious foyer. He scanned the living room, which lay in the stillness of ultra modern furniture that looked like museum pieces. Louver blinds covered floor-to-ceiling windows. Sunlight reflected off marble and crystal. His gaze gravitated to the original Rothkos and Mirós on the walls. Sayen's knees felt weak.

"Whad-ya-think?" Campbell asked.

"Quit bragging, you rich fuck," Sayen said, and meant it.

Campbell punched Sayen's arm. "I knew you'd be jealous, you ghetto trash."

Halle finally let go of Sayen's sleeve. "Yeah, it's cozy, but so was the Bates Motel. Don't take any showers."

Sayen felt positively numb by the time Campbell led him into a spacious kitchen that seemed all granite and stainless steel. A middle-aged Chinese woman stood at the island wrapping wontons and placing them onto a tin sheet.

Campbell rushed to hug the woman. "I missed you," he said while lifting her off her feet.

"Aii-ya. You only miss my cooking." She glanced at Sayen as Campbell set her down again. "So, you finally bring one through the front door instead of sneaking him in the back? Good. You're a man now." She reached up and pinched Campbell's cheek.

"This is Sayen Hommet," Campbell said, waving a hand toward Sayen. "Sayen, this is Pearl. She's been caring for Halle and me since the crib. She makes a fabulous pepper-roasted crab and a great deal of trouble."

Pearl smiled while stepping closer to Sayen. "Hommet? You be Middle Eastern, and Muslim. Your family live here in America?"

Sayen shook his head. "I'm from Libya. My family lives in Tripoli."

"No matter. Come, sit; I made wonton soup."

"Muslim's don't eat pork," Sayen said.

"No problem. Is shrimp dumplings."

Sayen didn't need to be told twice. He could smell the spicy soup simmering on the stovetop. He recognized that glorious aroma by the way it made him feel: like the comfort of nestling into his mother's bosom on the back porch at sunset.

"Pearl, can you make us sandwiches?" Campbell asked. "It's such a lovely day I thought Hom and I could have lunch on the beach."

Sayen felt his chest fall. Who the hell wanted white-bread sandwiches when this delightful woman could make them authentic Chinese cuisine? "No need to put yourself out on my account."

"Pearl doesn't mind, do you, old girl?" Campbell asked.

"Aii-ya. Not home two minutes and already making demands," she said, clucking her tongue. "I must make dumplings for party!"

Sayen's hopes raised the width of an eyelash, but he saw the tenacious line to Campbell's jaw. Giving up hope, Sayen said, "I can wrap dumplings. My mother taught me to be pretty handy in the kitchen."

"It's settled," Campbell said, closing the issue. "Hom, you help Pearl while I go have a heart-to-heart with my folks. Pearl, is Dad at home?"

She waived a hand toward the beach. "Digging for clams. I tell him there are no clams here, but he wants chowder and does not listen. He thinks he is a Kennedy at Martha's Vineyard." She gripped Sayen's arm and leaned into him while dropping her voice. "Men in this family are stubborn as mules. They only listen to themselves."

Sayen nodded, and they shared a chuckle.

"I heard that," Campbell whined. "I'm going to find Dad and break the news. I'll be back soon."

Halle swept into the kitchen as Campbell marched out. Pearl grabbed her wrist and pulled her to the island. Halle shook her head. "I'm not hungry."

"Eat!" Pearl snapped. "You must feed baby. Besides, I add fresh ginger, is good for soothing chi, and new mothers need strong chi."

Halle held up her shopping bag. "Let me put this away first, then I'll come back and soothe my chi."

Sayen washed his hands at the sink and sat at the island. He scooped a mixture of chopped shrimp and leaks and ginger from a huge bowl and dabbed some on a wrapper, folded the wrapper in half, sealed the ends to form a pouch, and lay it on the sheet-pan.

Pearl nodded as she watched his technique and then busied herself making a picnic lunch. They worked in silence for a few minutes before Pearl asked, "Where you meet Campbell?"

"At medical school."

"You be doctor like Campbell?"

"Yes, a pediatrician."

Pearl let out a long and sorrowful sigh. "Too bad you not meet my son, Jet, before Campbell. You like him better, I think. He hardworking Chinese boy."

Bingo, Sayen thought. At least I have one ally in this household. He felt his confidence building as his fingers continued to wrap wontons. "Well, if Cam's parents throw a hissy fit, maybe you can introduce us."

Pearl didn't look up from her sandwiches. She merely nodded and lowered her voice. "Mr. Reardon will be okay, I think. Mrs. Reardon…." She held out her hand, shaking it from side to side.

"Halle gave me the lowdown on Mrs. Reardon," Sayen said. Pearl's eyes grew as large as goose eggs. She tried to signal Sayen to say no more, but he ignored her warning. "She writes cuddly children's books, but in private, she's some kind of psycho dragon bitch."

Pearl whirled around and busied herself, which confused Sayen. He felt an odd sensation that something was terribly wrong. He spun around to see a woman standing behind him, carrying a basket of fresh-snipped roses. She was tall and elegant, and seemed to have an unyielding composure. Her perfectly groomed auburn hair reminded Sayen of cotton candy. She arranged her cerise-linen halter dress and kicked off her Jimmy Choo heels without making a sound.

"Pearl, there's mud on my shoes." Marilyn's voice was perfectly modulated, with rounded vowels and nipping consonants, level and cold. "Can you clean them since you seem to have so much spare time?"

"Aii-ya!" Pearl barked, without turning to face her employer.

"Young man," Marilyn continued, "I do not pay you to gossip about me in my own home."

A furious flash of anger surged through Sayen, anger at himself for being so careless. "Oh God, I'm terribly sorry, Mrs. Reardon. But you'll be glad to know that you're not paying me."

Marilyn's eyebrows lifted. "I beg your pardon."

Sayen attempted a smile but could only muster a halfhearted grin. "I'm not the temporary help. I'm a friend of the family."

In a rush of forced gaiety, Marilyn said, "My apologies. I'm Marilyn, the psycho-dragon-bitch mother." She marched to the counter where a blue vase sat waiting.

"Pleased to meet you. I'm Sayen Hommet, the totally mortified boyfriend. I was raised in Libya, and I'm here on a student visa, but I plan to get a green card."

Marilyn scrutinized him from head to heels, seemingly too stunned to respond. When she finally spoke, she raised her voice and slowed her delivery. "Well, this is a shock. Don't worry, darling, it's a pleasant surprise, and I pay no attention to what Halle says about me these days."

"It's her way of saying that you're formidable," Sayen said.

Marilyn's smile widened as she half filled the vase with water from the faucet. "Who knows what goes through her head. As for you, I approve wholeheartedly." She began to arrange the cut roses into a bouquet as she glanced at him, half suspicious and startled, half amused.

"You do? That's a relief." Sayen shot a look at Pearl, who seemed confused, yet still guarded.

"You're a Muslim," Marilyn said, not as a question. "You speak English very well for a foreigner."

"As a boy, I worked in the bazaar, running errands for my father and fetching trays of tea for anyone with a few pennies to spare. I learned enough English, French, and Spanish to lure tourist to my father's carpet shop, then I would act as my father's interpreter. I became adept at bartering in several languages." Yes, he thought, it had been nearly impossible to learn this inflexible, insufficient, dreadful language, with its crude grammar, insufferable spelling, and harsh authoritarian sound. But after ten years of living in this country, he had not only learned it well, he had begun to dream in English. The agile beauty of his native language was a fading memory.

"A bazaar urchin, how charming. Do you habitate here in the city?" Marilyn asked.

Sayen shook his head. "Stanford, where I attend medical school."

"Your family must be affluent. Surely your father does more than sell carpets. Perhaps a bit of oil money?"

Sayen felt himself redden. The inquisition had begun. "No, actually, my family and I no longer correspond. I barely have two dimes to rub together. I'll be paying off student loans for the next millennium."

She stared at him for a moment, as if his response had been inappropriate. Her hair curled lightly around her face, and she brushed a strand from her eye. "My goodness, Prince Charming has no kingdom, how delightfully bohemian. How long have you two been dating?"

Halle breezed in and sat next to Sayen. Pearl placed a bowl of steaming soup in front of her.

"About seven months. Hard to believe, seems more like seven days."

Marilyn turned to give him an unabashed stare. After a moment of silence, she said, "Halle, don't sit so close to the microwave."

"Mother, it's not even on."

"Don't use that tone with me, young lady. In your condition it's better to be safe." Her eyes drew back to Sayen. "So, dating for so long a time, and I'm just now meeting you? Things were certainly different in my day. But it sounds like you've been swept off your feet, hard as that is for me to believe. Forgive me for asking darling, but are you the father?"

Sayen suddenly felt like the stool he was sitting on had been ripped out from under him. He cocked his head to one side, trying to catch up to a situation that had taken a wrong turn and left him behind.

"Pardon?" he asked.

Marilyn placed the last rose in the vase and arranged it for an inordinately long time. "Well, you can't blame me for wondering. I mean, she's seven months pregnant, and that's how long you've been dating. I merely assumed...."

Sayen felt himself take charge again. "Mrs. Reardon, you misunderstood. I'm dating Campbell, not your daughter."

Marilyn let out a delightful chuff of laughter. "Funny. It seems what our pauper prince lacks in finances he makes up for with wit."

"It's no joke, Mom," Halle said. "I'm your only source for grandchildren. So you better start treating me like I matter."

Marilyn's mouth opened, making a perfect, Maybelline-red zero. Every vein in her neck became visible. "Don't be ridiculous.

Campbell can't tell Prada from Payless. He hates opera, and he is notorious for his fashion faux pas. Even on the remote chance that he were gay, my Campbell would never date a...."

Pearl slammed a pot down onto the stove behind Sayen, which startled everyone. She raised her hands and rested them on her hips as she glared at Marilyn.

Marilyn stood speechless as full comprehension sank in. She moved a hand to her throat, as if choking off her rising anguish. "Excuse me while I place these on the dining room table." She grabbed the vase by the neck as if she were strangling a chicken, and glided from the room.

A silence settled over the room as Sayen wrapped dumplings and Halle slurped her soup. A minute passed before a sudden crashing sound from the next room made Sayen jump an inch off his stool. He and Halle traded glances.

"Now that's the reaction I expected on the first take," Halle said with a smirk.

Pearl shook her head and clucked her tongue. "That vase was Lalique crystal." She shuffled to the pantry and grabbed a mop and bucket. She shot Sayen a look as she left the room.

"She hates me," Sayen said. "I should have let Cam tell her."

Halle laid a soothing hand on his arm. "She'll get better, or at least calmer. She'll go to her room, pop some valium, and wash them down with Scotch. Don't look surprised. You're family now, might as well know our dark secrets."

"Not sure I need to know them all."

Halle smiled. "Well brace yourself, Sayen. In case you haven't figured it out, we're not the Von Trapps."

"My friends call me Hom."

"Hom. I like that. Call me sis."

They touched fists. Sayen's spirits lifted once more as he figured he was batting two for three with one to go. He dropped his head and continued to wrap wontons. "So what are your plans for the baby?" When Halle didn't answer, he glanced over to see her face had darkened; he had trod onto dangerous ground. "Come on, sis, you might as well give me all the secrets."

Halle sighed. "Mom arranged an adoption. The couple is middle-aged, Catholic, and right-wing. I absolutely gag at the idea of them being so Republican. I mean, I don't want to give it to just anybody, you know?"

"You want to keep it?"

"I don't want junior growing up to be an accountant or a dentist. But Mom says a stable family is what's best, and even when she's a cold-blooded shrew, she's usually right."

"There are other choices."

"It's way too late for that."

Pearl breezed into the room, shuffled to the cabinet, and dumped a mound of broken glass and roses into a plastic lined garbage can. Then she rung out the mop in the sink and stored it and the pail in the pantry.

Sayen said to Halle, "I meant a different couple, one you have a relationship with so you could help raise the baby. You know, be Auntie Halle."

"You are seriously fucking with my chi," Halle said.

"I'm only suggesting—"

"Look, I appreciate this whole flattery thing you're doing, telling me I'm beautiful and now offering to solve my adoption problems, but let me clue you in. I'm already sold. You make Golden Boy happy, so I'm happy. Save the schmooze for the folks. They're the ones you need to impress."

Sayen shook his head as his voice rose a few decibels. "I don't give a flying fuck whether you or your folks like me. Cam loves me and nothing will break us up. I asked because I'm genuinely concerned about you and the baby."

Halle's eyes dropped; she became still. "Sorry, it's been a long time since anyone was interested in what I want. Tell me something, do you believe in love at first sight?"

"You mean, the kind that lasts longer than a weekend?"

AT THE water's edge, Blake Reardon stood with his trousers rolled up to his knees, holding a pail and shovel. His face had fallen, and the color had drained from it. Campbell pulled his gaze away from his father, not able to face the shock etched so clearly in those eyes. He stared across the heat shimmering off the sand to the edge of the bay. There were a few kids playing in the surf, looking minute and white against the deep blue, and not so far off, he saw the orange bridge that had been a landmark of San Francisco for over half a century. He found strength in that bridge, standing tall and proud against the elements.

Blake staggered back a step or two, shaking his head. The movement brought Campbell's focus back on his father, and what he saw was a sad, older man who had been shaken to his foundation.

"I certainly didn't see that one coming," Blake said. "Does your mother know?"

Campbell raised his shoulders and let them drop. "I've never told her, but who knows what moms know or don't know?"

"I take it this young man is someone special?"

A feeling of sweet relief swept through Campbell's core. Somehow that question told him things would be fine, that his father would accept him, accept both him and Sayen. When he spoke, he could feel his excitement lifting his voice. "I've never met anyone even remotely like him, Dad. I love him, and I know you'll like him too."

Over the sound of the pounding waves, a gull shrieked. Campbell glanced up to see the bird in a slow motion ballet, whirling in a tight circle.

"Do you mind my asking if you're really gay," Blake asked, "or is this the kind of bisexual thing that the kids are doing nowadays?"

Campbell chuckled, his confidence growing by the moment. "Totally gone over to the dark side, Dad. I just didn't know how to tell you. I hope you're not hurt that I've kept it secret."

Blake stepped toward his son and laid a hand on his shoulder. "Hurt? No, I understand perfectly. But in your profession there are career and social repercussions if you live openly as a homosexual. Much as I admire you coming out to me, you need to keep this relationship private."

"That's funny, considering you're the one who taught me to never lie. It's killed me keeping it secret this long. I have no respect for people who live in the closet, and neither does he. We want to live like you, Dad: an open book, and let the world judge us as they may."

Blake squeezed his son's shoulder, perhaps a little harder than he intended. "Son, be reasonable. Everyone keeps secrets, even me. You're too young to realize how vicious people are."

Campbell brushed his father's hand from his shoulder. He could feel anger boiling up from his chest to fill his head. For the first time in a long time, his father was letting him down, going against what he knew was right and just. "The only way we'll ever change the world is by defying all you bigots by living openly."

"I'm not a bigot, and I won't stand for you calling me that." The shock on Blake's face made him look like he had just been slapped. "But you've got to know that you can't change the world by flaunting your relationship in everybody's face. That may be fine at the university, but once you're in the professional world, like it or not, things are still governed by the good-old-boy network."

"Dad, even if I agree to hide it, he never would. He's not capable of hiding anything."

"Son, listen to me. You've got to—"

"No! I won't listen. You're wrong. I love you, Dad, but you're as wrong as you can be. We will change this world, even if we have to bury every one of those fucking bigots under the dead weight of their own ignorant hatred." The rush of energy surging through Campbell made him feel as if he were on fire. This defiant pride was unexpected, something new, something he knew came from the strength of his relationship with Sayen. *Yes,* he thought, *together we're strong. With this power, I can be my own man in this unjust world, and screw whoever doesn't like it.*

"Okay, okay, calm down," Blake said. "I'm just trying to save you from a lot of pain. But it seems you're determined to learn that on your own. Come on; tell me about him while we walk back to the house."

This victory caused the power surging in Campbell to jump to a new level, leaving him light-headed. He looped his arm over his father's shoulder as much to steady himself as to bring them closer, to reform the bond between father and son. "He's a year behind me at school. Dad, he's honest and caring. And when he holds me, we fuse into one person. I've never felt so safe with anyone."

"Well, now I really must meet him." Blake let out a laugh that carried a note of pure joy.

"You'll only have a few hours to get to know him. We're flying to Thailand for two weeks before our next semester starts. Our flight leaves at midnight."

Blake laughed again. "This is sounding more and more like Cinderella all the time."

CHAPTER EIGHT

FOR the first time in years, Blake felt a close, resilient bond between Campbell and himself. The thought had never occurred to him that his son would turn out gay, that there could be so much of himself captured in that young, vibrant, beautiful boy he had loved so much, perhaps too much. The idea of it made his head swim in a sea of delicious emotions. The urge to bear-hug his boy, to hold his son to his breast and feel their hearts beating together became overpowering.

The past seven months, since Blake's last lover dumped him, he had wallowed in loneliness and self-pity. It had been a bitter time for him, a time when he had been driven to the point of giving up altogether—on life. His son's confession came as a burst of bright sunlight after a black and violent storm. He felt elation surging through him, and he couldn't wait to meet this young man who brought joy to his son's heart.

He followed Campbell into the kitchen, noting the spring in his son's step, seeing how Campbell lit up the room with energy. Campbell crossed the room to a young man who had his back turned to Blake, someone whose shape was vaguely recognizable. Campbell laid a hand on his lover's shoulder. "Hom, I'd like you to meet my father, Blake." Campbell turned to his father. "Dad, this is Sayen Hommet."

The young man turned. Blake looked into those familiar blue eyes, and his heart froze. For the rest of his life, especially during those dark hours of staring at the ceiling while waiting for the sun to rise, Blake would look back on that moment as a turning point. That moment, because the instant before was the last time he could pinpoint as being himself. Normal. Somewhat happy, nothing going through his head except experiencing the joy that radiated from Campbell. It wasn't that after that good things didn't happen, happy things, mundane things—sipping coffee in the early morning, making love, getting ready to go out on the town, whatever. But everything else in his life would be colored by what he saw in that face, the face of the lover who had dumped him several months earlier. It was as if Blake had strolled into that kitchen to share his son's joy, and someone else, someone entirely different, staggered away.

Blake and Sayen stood a few yards apart, staring at each other, both unmoving, eyes wide. The shock imprinted on Sayen's face matched the panic that Blake felt moving from his gut to his throat. He struggled to force air past that solid lump of panic lodged in his windpipe. Seconds ticked by like hours.

Sayen sported jeans and a pullover shirt, very casual, and he wore them in such a way as to seem a god descended from Olympus. His manly posture, radiant skin tones, and fatally blue eyes all brought back Blake's hunger for this man that he had suffered all these long months.

"Did you hear me, Dad?" Campbell asked. "I said this is Sayen, my boyfriend."

Enough of the situation sieved through the fog of Blake's shock that he knew he should step forward and shake Sayen's hand as if they were meeting for the first time. But his shoes had somehow become nailed to the floor. He couldn't coax his legs to move.

"Okay," Campbell said, "you two are freaking me out. What gives?"

Blake somehow managed to suck in a lungful of air. His voice trembled as he spoke. "I... I... I'm sorry, son. You told me you had a boyfriend, but it didn't sink in until I saw him standing there."

"Ditto," Sayen mumbled. "I've never met a father-in-law before. I'm… overwhelmed."

Blake managed to step across the room when Sayen held out his hand. But Sayen wasn't offering his hand to shake. His fingers were curled except for the index, which pointed at Blake's feet. "Nice look, Mr. Reardon."

Blake glanced down, only to realize his trousers were still rolled up to the knees from digging for clams in the surf. A wave of heat washed over his face. He desperately wanted to bend over and roll his pant legs down, but that would have been even more embarrassing. The realization that this man who had stood at the center of his universe was making fun of him, stung in a way he had never felt before, because it defined a new set of boundaries for their relationship moving forward.

Blake stuck out his arm, and Sayen took his hand, shaking it tenderly. The joy of touching this soul again made Blake's eyes mist. A warm sensation of longing threaded its way through each finger and raced up his arm. Sayen tried to pull his hand away, but some part of Blake refused to let go. He held on, until the moment grew even more awkward.

The edges of Sayen's lips curled upward into a glorious smile. That lighthearted beam made Blake forget everything else at that moment, transporting him to the verge of tears. He felt his knees liquefying, and he was suddenly sure he would fall over. He steadied his grip on Sayen, to keep himself on his feet. It was the most magnificent and terrifying moment of his life.

Campbell laid his hand on Blake's forearm. "Dad, what's wrong?"

Blake, pulling himself out of a state of shock, released Sayen's paw and rubbed his hand over his chest. That hand tingled, as if from lack of circulation, yet was warm and pulsing as it covered his heart. "I'm sorry. Did you say father-in-law? Have you two tied the knot?"

"Not yet, Dad," Campbell said.

"Look on the bright side, Pop," Halle said. "You always wanted two sons."

Blake hurled a glance at his daughter that could freeze mercury. He turned back to Sayen. Those eyes, those pensive eyes that seemed as deep as space stared back at him. Blake felt his insides disintegrating. He managed another deep breath. "I'm pleased to meet you, Sayen. Welcome to our family."

"Likewise, Mr. Reardon. That is your correct name, right, Blake Reardon? Or should I just call you Dad?"

Blake floundered for a response. He struggled to concentrate, but his mind refused to engage further. He had always demanded the position of being in charge, the man holding the puppet strings, and he had always been haunted by worries of not being in control, yet now he found himself in a situation that was beyond his ability to grasp, let alone manage. His two separate planets of "upstanding family life" and "forbidden lust" had somehow collided, and he couldn't see anything past the mass of shimmering, cosmic debris.

He mumbled a feeble apology and stumbled from the room to beat a path to the first-floor toilet. The bathroom door opened and then closed with a hollow sound as it bounced back from the frame. Everything in the universe seemed to carry on as usual; every law of nature was still intact, yet inside Blake, everything had broken.

He sank onto the cold tile, hugged the closed toilet, and tried to cry. He couldn't.

Blake pressed his face to the cool porcelain for what seemed like only moments before he heard a sharp rap at the door, followed by Marilyn's voice. "Blake, darling," she said, "I'd like a word with you in my study."

How could he possibly face her now? But then, Blake had no other choice. There was nothing else he could possibly do except pull himself off the floor and confront her, confront each of them, all the while praying for strength.

He struggled to his feet and—avoiding the mirror over the sink because he couldn't look at himself yet—opened the door. Marilyn appeared at the doorway looking as if she had downed a few stiff shots.

"So they've told you," she said. "I can see you're as shaken as I am."

Blake found his voice. "I'm fine."

"I've seen you fine. What you are right now is nowhere near fine. Come to my office. I'll pour you a Scotch." She marched away and he followed.

When she handed him a tumbler of whisky, she said with a softer, almost frail voice, "I never dreamed this was possible, Blake. It never once entered my mind."

She turned her back on him as he took a long swallow. A burn traveled all the way to his gut; then the familiar numbness hit his head, lifting, lifting, lifting his hopes that he could find a way out of this train wreck.

"Blake, we can't let this boy lead Campbell astray. He's confused. He needs our help."

The way she spat the word "boy" felt like a knife plunging into Blake's chest. He felt the overpowering urge to defend Sayen, defend both the boys he loved. "Sayen isn't leading him anywhere he doesn't want to go. Besides, he told me that Sayen is not his first lover. Face it, our son is gay, and he could do a lot worse than Sayen."

Marilyn whirled around. Her voice honed itself into a knife-edge. "We must do something. He's a Muslim for God sake. I'm not about to endure our friends' gossip."

"I can see where that would be an issue," he said with dripping sarcasm.

"Dammit, Blake. This is no joke. This will ruin your bid for a senate seat. I know we haven't talked about it, but I'm not stupid. For years you've been positioning yourself to run for office."

"Don't be ridiculous. In this state, having the gay vote behind me can only help. Besides, what can we do? Campbell's not a child, and he's convinced he loves this man."

Marilyn poured herself two fingers of whisky in a tumbler and knocked it back. Her shoulders seemed to relax slightly. "Yes, I see your point. But we can't just sit back and let our son ruin his life and ours. There are clinics that can change him, make him normal."

"Don't even go there. He is what he is, and we'll support him no matter how much it hurts."

"The hell we will!"

Blake's hand involuntarily rose, but he stopped it. It was a natural reaction to the thought in the back of his head, the one that wanted to bitch slap Marilyn into next week. His hand twitched, craving release. Just one little satisfying slap was all it required. Blake saw it happen in his mind, the stunned look on her face as she fell back into the armchair, the stupefied silence, the realization that he did not, could not, share her animosity. He turned his back to her, stuffing his hand in his trouser pocket and wiping the image from his mind.

He polished off his Scotch and set the glass on Marilyn's desk. He considered pouring himself another but thought he should keep a clear head.

"Have Matt Hitchman run a background check," Marilyn said. "I don't trust him. I don't. Who knows what he's after?"

"There's no need for that. He's a good kid, I know."

"How, dear? How could you possibly know? We can't go by what Campbell says. He can only see stars."

"Because Matt ran a check on him over two years ago."

"You knew about him and you didn't tell me?"

Blake hesitated, surprised by his own stupidity. "I suspected something. I didn't know for sure until today."

Marilyn's eyes narrowed. "How could you know two years ago? Sayen said they've known each other only seven months."

Blake pulled a handkerchief from his pocket and dabbed his brow. "Did I say years? No. It must have only been a few months. I'm so damned confused I don't know what I'm saying." Blake glanced around the room, looking for an escape route. Just when he thought things couldn't get worse, he found himself falling further into hell.

"What did Matt find out?"

"His mother brought him here from Libya to attend school. He's here on a student visa. She worked as a secretary to pay for his schooling. He apparently had a rather abusive father and brother back in Tripoli. I don't think he has any intention of going back."

"A family of hoodlums."

She used the word hoodlums, but Blake knew by her tone she meant terrorists.

"He's a straight-A student at Stanford Medical. I admire his determination."

"A gold digger. Poor Campbell."

"No, ambitious, perhaps. But he's a good kid."

"How could Campbell be so blind?"

Blake's hand began to twitch again. Just one little slap. "Apparently he's obsessed with helping underprivileged children. He's volunteered to spend two years with Doctors Without Borders after he completes his internship."

"Doctors without money is more like it. What if he convinces Campbell to crawl through the damned jungle, or even worse go to some war-torn, Muslim shithole? We've got to stop this now."

"The Peace Corps didn't do me any harm," Blake huffed.

"I simply don't understand you. Our boy is being duped into financing this lark, and you're all smiles and admiration for this... this...."

"Trust me. I'm not happy, and I will do something. I just don't know what." He shuffled to the window and caught a glimpse of movement in the driveway. The boys, now shirtless, were shooting hoops at the side of the garage. Blake watched, transfixed, as Sayen glided with athletic grace and mongoose-fast reflexes. He dribbled while backing into Campbell, inching toward the basket. Sayen's butt pressed into Campbell's crotch while Campbell's hands swarmed over Sayen's skin. Like watching a surfer frolicking on a wave, the man was summer made flesh, freedom wrapped in a nimble package and dripping with sweat.

Blake focused so intently that all else smudged into pixels, with Sayen's face at the center. The hand in Blake's pocket unconsciously rubbed his crotch while observing this sexual display. He leaned forward until his nose touched the glass.

Behind him, Marilyn continued to yammer, but he no longer heard a word. He sank into a spellbound haze, watching Sayen shuffle, dribble, and shoot in a slow-motion ballet. He was poetry, the splendor of youth, the binding force of Blake's being. Sayen began to glow with a burnished light. He stared directly at Blake with an expression that promised all things: lust... love... redemption....

Blake flinched with a spasm of intense pain in his shoulder. He gasped for breath, grabbing his shoulder. He tried to massage the pain away until a harsh voice pierced his awareness.

"Blake! Have you heard a word I've said?"

Blake's spasm subsided. When the pain did not continue, he ignored it, just as he ignored Marilyn. He took a deep breath, blinked a few times, and continued scrutinizing Sayen.

CAMPBELL dribbled the basketball and shot for the hoop attached to the garage. Sayen recovered the ball.

"So, what do you think of them?" Campbell asked.

"Halle is hot. I love her already."

Sayen made his shot and missed. Campbell snatched the ball before it bounced. They danced around each other, weaving and blocking.

"Didn't I tell you she's the best of us?"

"Your dad's cool, but I'm sure he'll make trouble. And your mom, wow! She glared at me like a hangman measuring my neck size."

"Wasn't it strange how Dad froze when he saw you and then just ran out of there? I've never seen the great Blake Reardon at such a loss."

"They're in there talking about us," Sayen said. "Wish I knew what he's telling her."

"I mean, he was cool about my being gay until he saw you. Maybe it's because your skin is a shade too ethnic? Or because you're a Muslim? I just didn't figure him for that."

Campbell prepared to shoot, but Sayen wrapped his arms around Campbell, eye to eye; their foreheads pressed together.

"I'm worried they'll turn you against me," Sayen said.

Campbell smiled. "This from the man who said he would charm their socks off? Are you doubting your charisma?"

"I said that before I realized that I'm down by ten with only a minute left."

Sayen leaned forward and they shared a kiss, long, passionate, giving.

Campbell pulled back. "Personal foul." He jerked to the side and dove around Sayen, racing in for a layup. Sayen leaped at him, gazelle-like, and knocked the ball away. It soared toward the Bentley, bashing into the windshield. Crack! It bounced away, leaving a spider's-web fracture in the glass.

Sayen glared at the windshield. "Oh shit!" He glanced at Campbell, whose face had lost all its color. He looked frightened, Bambi caught in the headlights.

The front door of the house flew open, and Blake ran to the Bentley, gaping at the damage as if his child had been shot dead.

"My bad, Mr. Reardon," Sayen said. "I'll pay the repair bill."

Blake, seething, whirled around to face Sayen. But before he spoke, he visibly struggled to calm himself. Sayen braced himself. His stomach did a slow somersault in the silence while he waited for the explosion.

"No problem, Sayen," Blake said, finally. "An accident. I saw it from the window. Besides, that's what insurance is for. Right, Campbell?"

Campbell's mouth fell open.

"I'm so embarrassed," Sayen said. "It's such a beautiful car."

Blake lifted a hand and laid it on Sayen's shoulder. "Yes, it is. I felt guilty for buying it at first. But then I decided it was a midlife crisis, so that made it okay."

"You're so lucky. It must be a dream to drive."

Blake managed a nod. He squeezed Sayen's shoulder. "Would you like to drive it? We can take it to the body shop and get an estimate. Give us a chance to talk."

Campbell gasped. He had been speechless up to that point, but now he looked on the verge of fainting. Sayen felt somewhat amused and somewhat sorry for his young lover. "You bet, Mr. Reardon. I'd love to."

Blake had already begun to run for the house. He called over his shoulder, "I'll just grab the keys."

Sayen moved to Campbell and laced his arms around his bewildered lover's waist.

"What the hell is going on?" Campbell mumbled in Sayen's ear as he pressed himself to Sayen.

"I think he likes me."

---⟨⟪⟫⟩---

CHAPTER NINE

"WHAT the fuck were you thinking?" Blake screamed. He watched Sayen's fingers tighten their grip on the steering wheel, guiding the Bentley down a busy avenue as they drove toward downtown. Blake's shock and anger still had a stranglehold on his intellect, but being alone with this man again, after being convinced he would never see him again, had his emotions chortling. A confusing mixture of elation and rage had every nerve ending sizzling.

"How the hell was I supposed to know... Mr. Smith!"

"This is too colossal for coincidence; you had to know. The odds are billion to one that a father and son would randomly fall in love with the same man." *But how could he have found out?* Blake wondered. *I've always been so careful.* And in his heart, he refused to believe that Sayen was remotely capable of such a devious trick. *No,* he thought, *this boy would never do anything so underhanded. He is simply not a vindictive person.*

"If you had really loved me, you wouldn't have kept me in the dark with that fake name."

Love, not had loved, Blake thought. *No past tense. I've loved two men in my life, and I will continue loving both until they drop my dead ass in a coffin.* "Of course I gave you a phony name. I'm a federal judge, for Christsakes. You could have blackmailed me."

Sayen laughed, and gave the horn a toot for the hell of it. "Ha! That figures. I'm surprised you didn't have a bailiff come into our hotel room and say, 'All rise.' And as far as blackmail is concerned, no need to worry now, Dad."

"Stop calling me that. I don't approve of this."

"Remind me about the part where I give a rat's ass about your approval."

"If you hadn't walked away—"

"I didn't walk, Dad, I ran."

Blake turned his head to stare out the window. Sayen pulled the car to a stop at a red light, and they waited in silence. The air seemed thick, too dense for this climate. When the light turned green, Sayen eased the Bentley through the intersection and picked up speed. Blake continued to watch the people strolling along the sidewalk, but not really focusing on any one of them. They became a blur, exactly like the thoughts streaming through his head.

"We had something special," Blake mumbled while watching the pedestrians, not daring to look Sayen in the eye. "We could have been happy. As happy as it is safe to be in life." But then he realized that Sayen needed more than happiness. This young god wanted respectability, position, admiration. All the things Blake couldn't give him as long as he chose to keep his marriage together. For the first time he saw clearly into Sayen's core.

"Blake, will my marrying Cam ruin you?"

Blake's eyes closed tight as a jolt of acute pain shot up his arm. He grabbed his shoulder, trying to ease the throbbing. His breath grew ragged as he breathed through his mouth, but it seemed more like sucking air through a straw. He couldn't fill his lungs. His head began to spin.

Sayen let out a loud and joyous laugh.

Blake whirled around to see Sayen smiling at him, simply smiling, eyelids crinkled above and below those irises the color of a sapphire sky. "What's so damned funny?"

"On our last date, you told me you'd buy me a condo, pay my bills, take care of me. Well, you're gonna do all that and more, only it's Cam who gets the dessert while you pick up the tab."

As soon as Blake's eyes were back on Sayen, the shoulder pain began to ease into a dull ache. He rubbed his arm, soothing it more. "Funny! You're a regular fucking riot. That's right, laugh it up. We'll see who laughs last."

"Old Muslim wisdom: when God wants to punish you, he answers your prayers, only never the way you imagined."

"Don't think for a second that I'm letting you and Campbell remain lovers. Yes, I'll set you up and pay the bills. I'll even get you a country club membership if you want to be so damned respectable, but it's you and me from here on out."

"You're in no position to make demands."

Blake flung Sayen a gaze of uncompromising dominance. "I'm the money, remember? Money is always in the commanding position."

CAMPBELL paced the patio decking while Marilyn sat in a teak-and-brass deckchair under a blue-and-white-striped fabric umbrella, gazing with a basilisk stare at the Golden Gate Bridge gleaming red under the noonday sun.

She looked so formidable in her handsomely tailored linen suit and holding her wineglass like a scepter. She had that air of leisure and good health and abundance, the smugness of people who can't conceive of wanting anything more than what they already have. But something was not right with her. People have a rhythm, born from an internal vibration, and it is as unique as one's fingerprints. Campbell knew his mother's character by the tenor of her voice, like a calf knows the blazes on its mother, but just now that tone was different, loathsome, something he had never experienced from her.

To bolster his courage, Campbell visualized his lover's face as he last saw him. Sayen's face had radiated joy—like some dazzling light from deep within that couldn't be held back by mere flesh—as he pulled away from the house driving the Bentley. A kid with a new toy, or perhaps a voyager who realized he had finally arrived.

"I get that you're shocked," Campbell said. "This is a lot to throw at you all at once." He still felt unsteady, and he needed to keep moving to help keep his balance. Twelve steps to the railing, turn, twelve more back to the barbecue grill, turn, repeat, repeat. He had assumed his father would be the one objecting, and he'd also assumed he could count on his mother's support. He now struggled to understand how he could have been so wrong.

"Shocked is hardly an adequate word," Marilyn snapped. When she tapped the wineglass, her nails made a sound like a wind chime in a cold draft.

Worse than being wrong, of realizing that he underestimated both his parents, lay the knowledge that his mother refused to support him. He felt lost without her encouragement. She had always sheltered him, fought for him. They had that special bond only a mother and her firstborn can achieve. "Why is it perfectly fine for you to love a man but so wrong for me? And don't feed me that religious crap. You're no more devout than I am, since we both know that no just Creator would condemn His children to eternal hellfire for possessing hungers that He created in them." She was still sitting in the same unchanged position, and he made himself grin at her, drawing his lips back tautly across his teeth. She did not see it, refusing to look his way. "Now would He?"

Marilyn lifted herself out of the chair and strolled to the deck railing, still denying her son so much as a glance. "Do you have any idea what your life will be like?"

Campbell stopped a yard behind her, talking to the back of her head. "Yes, Mother, and for the first time, with him, I'm not afraid."

She glided several steps away, as if she were uncomfortable being that close to him. "You dated Pamela Evens all through high school and premed. How could you change in so short a time?"

Campbell trailed her like a lost puppy, and stopped a foot from her rigid back. He pulled his inhaler from his pocket, pressed it to his mouth, and gave himself a blast. "Mother, Pam's a lesbian. We used each other as cover."

"What a perfectly dreadful thing to say. She's a sweet girl. You had feelings for her." Marilyn strode a few feet farther away. She curled her hands into fists.

"Mother, I'm not doing this to hurt you. I love him. I can't help it."

"I don't believe that for a second. I won't believe it. You can change. While you were playing ball with that—"

"His name is Sayen."

"While you boys were playing, I phoned a friend, a therapist. She told me of a clinic in Monterey. It's called Straight To Heaven. They make people normal again."

Campbell ran his fingers through his closely cropped hair; an ache spread up his wrist and arm. He felt it stiffen his shoulder and solidify down his spine. Every part of him seemed to congeal—guts, glands, organs, bones. His lips jerked like a fish on a line while he stood in the midst of his own petrification, hating her, hating himself. In all his twenty-five years, he had never had the nerve to stand up to her, but he knew if he didn't do it now, he would lose everything he cared about.

"Mother, being heterosexual is not normal, it's just what most people are, which makes it common. Think of me as uncommon rather than abnormal. And don't use the word 'again.' I have never been straight."

Marilyn strolled a few steps farther away, her arms tight around her chest.

"Mother, I get that you're disappointed, but Sayen is what makes me happy."

"Yes, I can see he's smart as well as virile. Lucky you, to be allowed to enclose yourself on the erect pride of such virility."

"Mother, it's much more than physical, and it's not at all becoming to be so crass."

Silence.

"Mother?"

More silence.

"Mother, you can't just shut me out. It's not fair."

Marilyn whirled around, her eyes suddenly red, her face tight with anger. "Don't tell me what I can and can't do in my own house," she said, her voice a dozen decibels higher than before. She visibly struggled to compose herself. "My point is, rather than fly off to Thailand with this... with Sayen, I want you to stay here and seek professional help."

Campbell rushed to stand directly in front of her. She tried to turn away, still not able to look him in the eye, but he grabbed her arm and held her until her eyes lifted to meet his.

"You want me to marry some girl that I have no sexual interest in, a girl I can't love? Regardless of my pain, what kind of life would that be for her? What would she feel every time I stare at men on the street, or when I can't make love to her for months at time? Do you think I could subject a woman to that kind of lonely tragedy?"

Marilyn's mouth closed into a knot. Her eyes pooled with tears as she shook her head. She held a look of introspection rather than anger, as if she were examining her own life like a virus under a microscope, and not at all content with what she saw.

"I'm happy with him. For the first time in my life, truly happy. If you're struggling to accept us, then perhaps you should seek professional help."

She slapped Campbell, hard, and then her hands flew to her own mouth.

Campbell's hands fell to his side, hanging loosely. He felt his lips tighten into a thin, bloodless line. He stomped away and Marilyn followed.

"Campbell, I'm sorry. I didn't—"

"It doesn't matter," he said with a surprisingly calm voice.

"Of course it matters. Look at me."

He refused to turn around. He kept his head held high, staring off at a point at the Marin Headlands across the entrance to the San Francisco Bay. That was the first time in his memory that she had ever raised a hand to him, and the sting went all the way to his marrow and traveled through his skeleton like a vibration through a tuning fork. At that moment, something began to rise to the surface, something long buried in his heart—pure hate. It was a concept so foreign to him that he had no idea what these emotions could be. All he knew was it felt like a consuming rage directed at the one person in his life that he knew he should only love.

"Campbell, that boy is a guttersnipe who wants to be one of us."

Campbell's shoulders dropped. He looked down and gave himself another blast from his inhaler. "I'm so repulsive it's unthinkable that he actually loves me? Has it been so long since you loved Dad that you've forgotten what it's like to cherish someone?"

Marilyn stood silent for a long time. Campbell still had his back to her, so he could not tell if his blunt question had sent her into shock, or if she were merely composing herself for her next volley. He heard her swallow.

"Answer me honestly, would he be with you if you were penniless?"

Right, he thought, *with her it comes down to money and position*. He was seeing this side of her for the first time, but he realized that it had been there all his life. He only now noticed it.

"Yes, Mother, let's be honest. Would I be with him if he were an old troll?"

Marilyn reached for him. She ran her hand across his shoulder, caressing his neck. Her touch felt icy, and he moved away.

"Campbell, darling, I see that you love him, and I do remember what that's like. But as far as he is concerned, I've met the type before. He's using you."

Marilyn stepped in front of him, touched his chin, and lifted his head until their eyes met. Campbell yanked away, unable to maintain eye contact. He was afraid to let her see the hate boiling up in him. "This isn't about him," Campbell said. "It's about controlling me."

Even without looking, he could feel her posture going rigid, and he knew he had hit the bull's-eye.

"Darling, I'm simply pointing out that, apart from being ornamental in a somewhat vulgar way, this boy has nothing to recommend him. He will only hurt you. If you must fall for a boy, at least pick one of your own class."

"Christ, Mother, if you could only hear yourself. You sound like such a—"

"Darling, I am prepared to do whatever it takes to show you the kind of man he is. If you get on that plane tonight, I will cut off your allowance. We'll see how long he sticks by you when they repossess your car and refuse to honor your credit cards. Don't look at me like that; it's better to be hurt now than years down the road."

The rage in him seemed to burst, which threw him into a calm silence. That feeling that had remained hidden for so long—hate for his mother—stood clearly visible at the front of his mind like a flickering candle held close to the eyes. He felt a jolt of shock, but at the same time a composed acceptance. Knowing his true feelings gave him power over her.

He cleared his throat. "I know what I'm getting into."

"You're a boy who doesn't know what it's like to have the life crushed out of you by someone who doesn't love you. And I pray to God I never have the opportunity to say I told you so."

Campbell had already begun to march back into the house, leaving her on the patio. "Like you would let that opportunity slip by," he called back, playing his role with an ardent sense of the dramatic, which he didn't really feel. He did not look around, but he felt her stare on the back of his neck. He imagined her moving to the doorway, leaning against the jamb with one hand propped against the other side, as if barring him from returning. He refused to look, but he saw in his mind's eye the tragic picture of his figure moving away from her, as if it were him standing at the door watching his exit. The strange thing was, he had never loved nor hated her more than in that moment. *Fuck them all*, he thought. *They do not want me to find myself in them, they want me to lose myself in them. Or are they trying to find themselves in me, and don't like what they find?* For years he had been trying to find himself, in bars, in classrooms, in mirrors, in love, especially in love, for that self that is buried deep within every human being. He only caught glimpses of that self when he held Sayen close, and he realized that love was more than surrendering yourself to someone, it was also finding yourself in the surrender. It was only when he had walked out the front door that he let himself feel an appalling sense of loss.

HALLE sat at the island in the kitchen, chopping onions. She wiped away a tear.

"You and Sayen hit it off," Pearl said. "Will he raise your baby?"

The jolt that hit Halle felt like a bee stinging the back of her neck. "Where did that come from? All he asked was whether I'd consider other options?"

Pearl flashed a knowing smile. "What did you think he mean? He wants to raise your baby, and have you help."

"No way he said that." Halle stopped chopping, wiped away another tear, and reached for a second onion.

"Girl, with men, you must peek under the covers. If man talks about your wellbeing, you betcha he's thinking about himself. Mark my word, girly, he want something from you, and it what's in your belly."

"That would be so freakin' cool. But Mom would never go for it."

"How long you dance to her tune?"

Jet Yip strolled into the kitchen from the garden entrance hauling a grocery bag. He carried himself with an ungainly youthfulness, as if he were still growing into his body, yet everything about Jet was hip—baggy denims, leather jacket, hair brushed back into a ponytail—everything except the warm glow in his eyes and the three-year-old girl, Shelby Yip, holding on to his hand like he was a life raft.

"Ma," Jet said, "I brought your grocery order. So what's the emergency that you couldn't wait for the store to deliver?"

Shelby ran to Pearl and threw her arms around Pearl's legs. "Grandma!"

Pearl scowled at Jet while she lifted her hands in a silent question.

Jet shrugged. "Arlene had a hot date, so I get to babysit."

"That girl," Pearl snapped. She lifted Shelby to her breast and gave her a loving kiss and hug.

"You raised her," Jet said. "I only manage the fallout." He made a beeline to Halle and gave her a brotherly peck on her cheek. "Hey, dude. What-up?"

"I want you to help with the party," Pearl said. "But you know how Mrs. Reardon feels about...." She nodded her head toward the child.

"Ma! What was I supposed to do? You know how Arlene is."

"Cam came out to the folks," Halle said, "and all hell's breaking loose. And get this, lover boy is a Muslim from Libya. Who knew Cam ate anything but white bread?"

"Whoa! What the fuck?"

"Jet! Don't say bad words." Pearl nodded toward the child again. "You talk like I teach you."

Halle flashed Jet a devilish grin. "And you'll spray your shorts when you see his boy toy. He's a total stunner, and I mean stunner with a capital 'S'."

Jet flinched. "Shut up, dude! I'm not into prayer rugs and dates."

"I want a boy toy!" Shelby whined. "I want a toy!"

"Uh, yeah," Halle sighed. "Mahmud Bey? Sanjay?"

"This is me ignoring you. Besides, you're the one who's dating Rachid, the wacko from Morocco," he said as he patted her swollen belly.

Halle laughed. "Me? How about Omar Sinan? You are so busted."

"Omar Sinan?" Pearl said, raising her voice. "You date Mrs. Sinan son? He forty years old and a married man!"

"Ma!"

Pearl eased Shelby to the floor. "I don't want hear no more. Take Shelby and your gossip somewhere else. I call your cell when I need you. And don't let Mrs. Reardon see...." She nodded at Shelby.

CHAPTER TEN

BLAKE and Sayen stood in the customer waiting area of Costa
Plenty Motors. On the other side of a glass window, a bald,
wrinkled-faced mechanic, looking much like a shar-pei dog,
estimated the damage to the Bentley, jotting notes onto a form held
to a clipboard. The smell of grease and dust and paint thinner
enveloped Sayen, but he didn't notice. His mind was redlining with
images of the country-club scene he saw so clearly in his near
future.

A high-pitched squeal brought Sayen's focus back to the
garage. At the other end of the room sat a man roughhousing with
his young son, who shrieked with joy as his father held him in a
headlock.

Sayen glanced at Blake, hoping to share the moment, but
Blake's eyes pooled with tears while staring at the father and son.
He seemed to be fighting back an emotional outburst. He took a few
deep breaths and wiped moisture from the corner of one eye. "It's
my fault. I mean, I must have rubbed off on him somehow."

"You're suggesting you passed him some kind of gay
chromosome?" Sayen asked, trying hard not to smile. "That you
emit some homo-causing pheromone?"

Blake shook his head. "I never took him to little league, tossed
a ball, or showed any overt affection. I was afraid that if I was found
out, then any kind of normal affection would have been
misinterpreted." He paused and took another deep breath, looking at

the grimy ceiling. "Hell, the truth is I was always too wrapped up in my own interests. I left all that to his mother."

Sayen gripped Blake's shoulder. "As long as he's happy, what's the difference? And with a little financial help from you, I'll keep him blissfully happy."

Another squeal of delight from the boy turned Sayen's head. He would have preferred swimming across an alligator-infested swamp than being sucked into Blake's self-pity. And right then, more than anything, he longed to wrestle his way into the middle of that joyous boy and his father and share in their happiness.

"You don't understand," Blake said. "These things are hard for me, hard even to talk about. I mean, I never...."

Sayen gave Blake's shoulder another gentle squeeze, rather than the shove he would have preferred. "The only thing to do is accept him and make him feel loved."

"It's not just him I'm worried about. It's me too."

Sayen sat back in his seat and fantasized about making love to Campbell, stroking that beautiful hard cock through virgin-white jockey shorts, progressing to breathless and sweaty lovemaking. He pictured Blake walking in on them, and Sayen not cowering, being proud, waiting for Blake to see the leer on his face before he turned his attention back to Campbell. He knew that vision had no chance of happening. Life never seemed to follow one's perfect desires without throwing in big chunks of reality separate from the vision. But the idea of Blake seeing firsthand what he could have had all to himself, had he had the courage, made Sayen's imagination sizzle.

Mr. Green, the mechanic, stomped into the waiting room, wiping his hands on the flanks of his overalls. He moved his huge, wrinkled face to within inches of Blake's face and offered Blake a handshake, then presented him with the estimate. Blake checked the bottom line and whistled. "It's a piece of glass for God's sake, not the fucking Hope Diamond."

"Right," Mr. Green said, "like I can just blow a windshield out of my ass and slap it in there. This has to be custom made."

Sayen said, "No worries, I said I'd pay for it."

Blake's face grew pink. "And whose deep pockets pay in the end?"

"You said yourself you have insurance. Why sweat the small stuff?"

Blake stormed out of the waiting room and stood beside the Bentley.

Mr. Green glanced at Sayen with an expression of melancholy. "Why are all these rich dudes such tightwads? It's like it's not enough that they have it all, they don't want anybody else getting any for themselves."

Sayen nodded. "He thinks having money is the only thing that makes him special."

Sayen stepped to the Bentley's driver door and opened it. He glanced over his shoulder at the father and son, still roughhousing, before he climbed into the driver's seat. The car was his again, he thought, as he took possession of the walnut steering wheel. The leather seat creaked beneath his weight, comforting him. It now carried the faint stench of the garage, and he couldn't wait to get his car and himself away from what had turned into a humiliating scene. He started the engine, eased the car to the edge of the road, and pulled into traffic.

Sayen drove fast but carefully, trying to put distance between them and the garage. For the first time since meeting Blake, the man had showed emotion about how much something cost. It made no sense to Sayen that this wealthy man would pay five hundred dollars for a bottle of wine at a restaurant without so much as raising an eyebrow, yet demean himself to a greasy mechanic over the cost of a windshield.

Sayen rolled his window down to clear the air inside of that garage odor, and focused on driving this luxurious machine. He waited for that feeling of satisfaction to return. It did.

They rode for several minutes in silence before Blake said, "What if I leave her? Would you give up Campbell? Would you live with me?"

Sayen tried to swallow, but his mouth had suddenly gone dry. "Are you mad?" he managed to say. "Give up your family, friends, social position? Do you think I would rob you of all that?" Sayen knew that seven months ago he would have jumped at it, but that was before developing a relationship with Campbell, and now with Halle. He knew he couldn't do this to them. It was unquestionably too late. Or was it?

Blake's expression fell into something painful. He held his chest, wheezing. When he spoke, his voice sounded funny, and had a desperate edge to it. "Watching you shoot hoops, I felt like I woke out of a twenty-five year coma. With you I'm alive. Nothing else matters to me."

Blake waited, studying him, demanding an answer with his eyes.

"You're proposing to me?"

"Agreeing to leave my wife is not enough—now you want me on one knee?"

HALLE sat on her bed in her bra and panties with Shelby sitting beside her. The afternoon sun spilled through the windows like golden honey. The room grew warm and fragrant. Halle tied colorful bows to the girl's long hair while Shelby used a hairbrush to style the wavy locks of one of Halle's Barbie dolls. Jet crouched on the floor sketching Halle's likeness on a drawing pad.

"He said he wants to raise your baby?" Jet asked.

Halle tossed her hair back and giggled. "In a roundabout way."

"I haven't even met him," Jet said, "and he's already my hero. Will you do it?"

Halle shrugged.

The ends of Jet's mouth lifted into a grin. "You've got a crush on your brother's boyfriend."

"Shut up. It's not like that."

Jet laughed. "You like, totally want to jump his bones. You slut!"

Halle looked away. She took the brush from Shelby and began brushing the child's hair.

"So," Jet said, "when you fantasize about him naked, is Campbell there too?"

"That's sick. Guys are so clueless."

"Jeez, you're friggin' radiant. Hold that pose." Jet ripped away the paper he had been drawing on and started a new sketch.

Thirty minutes later, Halle slipped into her mother's office. Marilyn sat at her desk, engrossed in the paperwork before her.

Halle coughed to attract her mother's attention before she said, "Now that we know Campbell isn't going to fertilize the family tree, maybe we should rethink the adoption?"

Marilyn didn't bother to lift her head from her paperwork. "Darling, I appreciate you trying to help, but let's not rock the boat any more than is absolutely necessary."

"But what if the delivery messes up my plumbing? This could be your only chance for a grandchild."

Marilyn finally lifted her head to stare at Halle, but her eyes seemed to glaze over. "And who will raise it? Your father and I are long past the baby-rearing years, and you're still a child."

"Pearl raised me and Cam. I could find someone to help. I mean, how tough could that be?"

"We have already decided, and I have gone to considerable trouble to find suitable parents and transact all the legal issues." Marilyn glanced back down at the papers before her, indicating that the discussion was closed.

"You mean you decided. You make decisions like nobody matters but you."

Marilyn slammed her fist down on the desktop. "I will not have my work undone. Look, darling, I appreciate you wanting to give us a grandchild. But you'll have others."

Halle stormed to the door and opened it. But before she left the room, she could not stop herself from getting the last word in. "I wasn't just thinking of you and Dad."

SAYEN slowed to a comfortable speed. He glanced at Blake and saw that the elder man was battling some inner conflict.

"I built my marriage on the basis of a sexual lie," Blake finally said. "I had known sexual fulfillment, love, once in the Peace Corps, but it ended quickly. All these years I believed I would never be fulfilled again, but then I met you. I'm a starved man, and you came along and offered me a banquet."

"More like raw meat to a lion." Sayen smiled, turning his attention back to the road.

Blake growled. He reached over and laid his hand on Sayen's thigh, giving it a squeeze.

"You're still building relationships on a lie," Sayen said. "To me, you were nothing more than a business transaction. You're starving all right, and it's made you delusional."

Blake started to answer quickly, dismissively, "That's not true. You were—" And then whatever he meant to say next caught in his throat like a finch fluttering to escape a cage. He glared at Sayen across a span of only two feet. Blake seemed stunned, and he was not an easy man to surprise. He seemed to fall back into that internal conflict, multiplied exponentially, yet tempered by his inner strength. "You were different. I always felt your passion for me. I still feel it."

Sayen opened his mouth to disagree, but he couldn't. He could not continue the lie or deny his feelings for Blake, but that didn't mean he would give up Campbell. There was no going back, even if Blake left his wife.

Blake scooted closer and leaned in to kiss Sayen. The younger man elbowed him away, but Blake seemed possessed. Sayen fought to keep the car under control. "Have you gone mental? Get off me."

A sharp yelp sounded outside the car, and the front fender lifted, as if rolling over a large bump. Sayen whirled around to look behind him. A burly man on the sidewalk screamed while bending over a limp dog. He lifted the dog to his chest and hugged it.

"Fuck!" Sayen stomped the brake pedal.

"Keep driving for God's sake," Blake gasped.

"We need to stop."

"I can't get mixed up in this. Quick, pull around the corner before he can get our license number."

When Sayen hesitated, Blake mashed his foot on the accelerator. The car picked up speed. Sayen checked the rearview mirror, only to find the burly man chasing after them, still clinging to his dog.

The Bentley rocketed forward, gaining speed. They approached an intersection, a red light staring down and a UPS truck entering crosswise. Sayen jammed the steering wheel to the right, and they swerved around the corner. The Bentley hurtled down the block before Sayen pushed Blake off the accelerator, braked, and pulled to the curb. "Dammit! We should have stopped to help."

Sayen checked the rearview mirror and saw the burly man, still clutching his dog, run around the corner and lumber down the street toward the parked Bentley. "It's not too late. We can go back."

"I'm not letting you mix me up in this scandal," Blake said. "Now get out and let me drive. I'm taking us home."

"It's not a scandal. It's an accident. They're called accidents because it's nobody's fault."

"It's not about the dog, you idiot. It's about driving around town with my gay son-in-law. What if some reporter decides to investigate?"

A sudden, loud crash made them both jerk their heads forward. The burly man held his dog in one arm while pounding his fist on the hood, making a sizable dent. The dog looked to be part collie, part anybody's guess. The man kicked the grill in a violent tantrum.

"Stay in the car," Blake said. He swung the passenger door open and stepped from the front seat, cautiously inching toward the dog owner. "Now see here, I'm terribly sorry we ran over your pet, but you should have had him on a leash. We are not at all to blame."

Sayen looked on in silence as the burly man balled up his hand and cocked his arm. He took three quick steps to Blake, whose face lit up in total surprise as he saw that massive fist whizzing toward his nose.

CHAPTER ELEVEN

THE Bentley parked inside the garage. Blake leaped from the passenger side, holding a bloodied hankie to his nose. Large red spots stained his shirt.

The driver's door flew open, and Sayen jumped out. "It's not my fault. I had to tell the truth."

Blake bristled. "What the hell do you know about truth?"

Campbell strolled through the garden, recovering from the argument with his mother. He stopped cold when he saw his father. "Thought you two went MIA on me. Jesus, Dad, what happened to your face?"

Blake waved him off.

"Come inside and let me treat that," Campbell said.

"Leave me alone!" Blake snapped. "I'll get a raw steak from Pearl." Blake stormed past his son and into the house.

Campbell turned on Sayen. "You hit my father?"

"I didn't touch him, Cam. You might say he had a run-in with a dog named Karma."

Sayen took Campbell into his arms and held him close. He pulled back and kissed his lover. "What a disaster. I should have let you drop me off downtown. Can we go somewhere where we can be alone?"

"If I get you away from here, will you tell me what the hell is going on?"

Sayen nodded, and Campbell tipped up his chin on two fingers and peered into his eyes, displaying a change in mood, happy, amorous. "Pearl made us a picnic basket. Let's change into shorts and eat on the beach while you tell me about this dog named Karma." Campbell bent slightly to press his parted lips to his lover's just long enough for Sayen to taste the sweetness of his tongue.

Sayen crushed his face into the soft of Campbell's throat. "Deal."

Twenty minutes later they lay together on a blanket near the water. It was one of those rare San Francisco days where the temperatures grew hot, and people flocked to the shore. In places the sand was completely covered with beach towels, seeming like a patchwork quilt or prayer rugs in a mosque. Lovers cuddled, families lounged, children ran shrieking into and out of the cold waves. On the narrow, cobalt opening to the bay cantered yachts, small sailboats with colorful sails, and even an occasional windsurfer. The waves broke with a noise like "hurrah, hurrah, hurrah."

The day's heat seemed to be trapped close to the vast and preternaturally clean stretch of sand, and the smell of suntan lotion lingered on the air. Sayen broke into a light sweat as he lay atop the blanket. Smiling, he stretched his legs, tucking an arm under his head while holding a sandwich with the other hand. A wicker picnic basket and a boom box sat at the blanket's edge. A yowl floated up from the box, Linda Ronstadt singing "Desperado."

Campbell wore a lime-green Speedo that modeled a thin scar across his left hip. His genitals made an impressive three-knuckled fist against the nylon, making him look even sexier than had he been naked. He knew the power of sexual seduction and handled it with ease. He lay on his side, propped on one elbow with his cheek sunk on the palm of his hand, watching Sayen chow down on the sandwich.

Sayen felt comfortable wearing nothing but a pair of Campbell's faded boardies. The hot sun on his skin felt as delicious as the tuna fish sandwiches. He looked up to see Campbell studying him over the top of his designer shades, with the look of a small boy viewing a grownup's movie he could not fathom. "What?" Sayen said with a mouthful of food.

"You eat with such relish. I love that about you. You're passionate about everything."

Sayen swallowed as he considered his lover's exquisite proportions. Campbell seemed so much more alluring being nearly naked in public. "You wear those trunks every time you hit the beach?"

"You like them? They show off my ass."

"They show off everything. But you need some tassels hanging from your nipples."

Campbell made a grimace, screwing up his face. "Shut up!" he said as he punched Sayen's arm.

Sayen laughed. "I can't believe your parents didn't know you're gay."

Campbell pounced on his lover. They grappled until they were tangled in the blanket. A fierce playfulness had them both laughing and struggling at the same time, taking pleasure in the sheer physical exertion, two lion cubs sparring. Sayen felt the hot sand burning his neck and back, which made him fight all the harder. They wrestled until their strength waned, and they lay exhausted, laced in each other's arms and legs, at peace.

Above the sound of waves pounding the sand, came the ending cords of the Ronstadt song, "*You better let somebody love you, before it's too late.*"

Campbell leaned over his lover's face and kissed those thin lips, a gentle, searching kiss.

Sayen responded. Both men breathed heavily. The sweetness of Campbell's breath was enthralling. Sayen glided a hand over that smooth chest and felt Campbell's heart pounding. It matched the violence of his own heart. He nuzzled this face into Campbell's shoulder and shut his eyes.

"Let's stay like this all day," Campbell said. "I love cuddling."

"People are staring."

"I don't care anymore."

Sayen glanced up and shielded his eyes from the sun's glare. A boy stood on the edge of the blanket staring at them, on the verge of tears. The kid couldn't have been more than three years old, had a thatch of tawny hair, and wore a rust-colored tank top and bright green shorts.

"Little brother," Sayen said, "are you looking for someone?"

The boy shook his head, no.

"What's your name?" Sayen asked.

The boy didn't answer. His chin began to tremble.

"Where is your mommy?" Campbell asked.

As the boy vaguely pointed down the beach, tears began to stream down his cheeks.

Sayen sat up, pulled a napkin from the food hamper, and dabbed the boy's face with it, telling the boy not to cry, that they would find his mother. The boy looked down, squeezing his eyelids together. Sayen wiped the snot from the boy's upper lip, then told the boy to blow, which he obeyed. Sayen pulled the napkin away from that red nose, but kept it ready should it be needed again. He gave the boy a comforting smile.

The boy, calmer now, cocked his chin upward and stared into Sayen's eyes. "You're not my brother."

"Are you sure?" Sayen asked, his smile growing wider. "How do we know for sure if you won't tell me your name?"

"Jamie. I'm Jamie, and my brother is Mark. He's six."

"Jamie's a nice name. My name is Sayen, and this is Campbell."

Jamie nodded.

Sayen knelt before the boy. "Jamie, I called you little brother because where I come from, we are all brothers, and because I always wanted a little brother just like you. Is it okay if I call you brother?"

Jamie nodded again.

"You don't talk much, do you, little brother? How about we go find your mommy. Would you like that?"

Jamie nodded again.

Sayen and Campbell stood and took hold of Jamie's hands. They meandered along the beach in the direction Jamie had pointed, with the boy between them. But when the boy began to dance on the hot sand, Sayen realized that Jamie had stood on their blanket to cool his feet. Sayen lifted the boy onto his shoulders, and the boy pressed his hands against Sayen's forehead.

"Can you see your mommy from up there?" Campbell asked.

Jamie shook his head, no.

"No problem, little brother. She must be here somewhere. We'll find her." Sayen felt the boy's warm legs clinging to his neck. He reached over and grasped Campbell's hand, interlacing their fingers. They ambled along at a slow pace, as if they were sightseers strolling through a comely seaside town, taking in the sites. Campbell would occasionally ask people if Jamie belonged to them, without success.

They came upon a couple sleeping on a blanket. She was a long-lined blonde lying full length, stretched out, her arms above her head, wearing a skimpy, leopard-skin bikini. Her tight little bra scarcely covered her small nubs of breasts, and her brief panties wrinkled enticingly between her closed-together legs. He, red-haired and hunky, had the kind of pasty skin that could never tan. He had that neat, groomed look that suggested military. They had both started to burn.

All of a sudden Jamie bounced on the back of Sayen's neck and slapped the top of his head, urging him on like a stubborn donkey. "Mommy!"

They stopped at the edge of the blanket. Campbell knelt and shook the man awake. When the man sat up and shielded his eyes from the glare, Campbell said, "I think we found something that belongs to you."

The man looked up as Sayen lifted Jamie from his shoulders and placed him on the blanket. The man's eyes slowly passed over

Sayen and Campbell. He grimaced and looked away. The boy shrank away from the man, who shook the woman awake. As she sat up, the man said, "The brat wandered off again. I told you to watch him. What kind of shitty mother are you, anyway?"

Sayen took a long moment to admire the man's defined body and handsome face. He wanted to feel some level of attraction to this stud, but there was no way he could ignore the man's obvious distaste for him and Campbell. Sayen could feel the animosity radiating from this man.

"It's not my fault," the mother snapped. "I told him to stay close. He never listens."

"Well make him listen, dammit," the man's voice rose almost to a shout. "And where did the other one run off to? Get your skinny ass up and go find him."

Jamie turned his back to them, looking up at Sayen with pleading eyes. Sayen reached down and ruffled the boy's wild thatch of hair. "You take care, little brother." Then both Campbell and he began to walk away. After only four steps, Campbell stopped and turned, glaring back at the stud. "You're welcome!"

They ambled back to their blanket in silence. Once they plopped down, Campbell dug out more sandwiches, but Sayen had lost his appetite. He stared back down the beach, seeing the boy, Jamie, sitting on the blanket, looking as if he had lost a puppy. The father—or boyfriend—made no attempt to play with the boy. The mother was MIA, no doubt still looking for her other son.

Campbell stuffed a wedge of sandwich in his mouth and bit off a hunk. Chewing with force, his eyes followed Sayen's stare. He pushed Sayen's shoulder, roughly. "You were drooling all over that guy," he said with a mouthful of tuna fish. "And you're still cruising him. That is so rude."

"I was watching the kid. I feel sorry for him."

"So now you think I'm stupid? That's not only rude, it's insulting."

"Now that you mention it, daddy is a stud," Sayen said, hoping to give his lover a good tease. "Did you notice his box? Man, I'll bet he keeps her happy at night."

Campbell swallowed and tossed the rest of his sandwich back into the hamper.

"Pervert."

"You're the one showing off your family jewels to everyone on the beach. Face it, I like to look and you, obviously, like to be looked at. We're a matched set."

"I won't dignify that with a response."

Sayen gave a low-pitched chuckle. "Cam, that guy was pure asshole. I'm not interested in him or anyone else. You can trust me."

"Trust you? So who gave you that diamond-studded watch?"

"Cam, you know as well as I do that I got that months ago, before I moved in with you. Take my word for it, that's nothing."

"Look, dammit, I know you're hiding something. If you're seeing someone else, I don't want to know about it, but don't cruise other guys right in front of me."

Sayen sat up, turning serious for the first time. He stared into his lover's wide eyes and let a few moments tick by as they listened to the pounding surf. "You mean to say that if I was seeing someone, or even had dated someone special, you wouldn't want me to tell you?"

"In a gay relationship," Campbell said, "how much can two men really tell each other? I mean, how much truth can there be without jeopardizing the relationship?"

"As much as you can handle. It all depends on how strong we are, and how much we care about each other."

MARILYN walked down the upstairs hallway. As she passed Halle's bedroom, she heard squeaking bedsprings coming from behind the door. She stopped, put her ear to the door for a moment, long enough for her eyes to widen as the possibilities of what was causing the sound floated through her mind. She flung open the door.

Jet and Halle sat on the floor at the foot of the bed admiring sketches while Shelby jumped up and down on the bed. Marilyn scowled as her hands rose to her hips.

Jet glanced up and frowned. "Busted."

Halle jerked her head around to stare at her mother. "Don't make a scene. We were just leaving."

"And just where do you think you're going, young lady?"

"To the beach, where we can get some privacy."

Marilyn stood stiff with anger and silent as stone as Halle pulled a few things together and stuffed them into a shoulder bag. Then she picked up a framed painting wrapped with a red bow, took Shelby by the hands, and led her and Jet out of the room and down the stairs.

Once the kids were out of sight, Marilyn continued down the hall to Campbell's room. She slipped inside and locked the door. After crossing to the window, she pulled the blinds shut, then stared at Sayen's clothes laid out on the bed. His wallet, keys, and watch lay on the nightstand.

She hurried to the bed, but hesitated. She turned away, took a few steps toward the door, and hesitated again. Drawn back to the bed, she picked through Sayen's pants pockets, but found nothing. She snatched his wallet and meticulously sifted through each compartment, studying every picture, each piece of paper. Again, she found nothing that would shed any light on this young man, nothing that would give her any leads, any ammunition to battle him.

She returned the wallet exactly as she found it. Then something caught her eye, Sayen's watch. Yes, the same brand she had given her husband, but how did this guttersnipe get the money for such an expensive watch?

She picked it up and read the inscription. Transfixed, her knees liquefied, and she crumpled to the bed. The entire universe grew deathly silent except for the ticking clock on the chest of drawers, which suddenly sounded like a bomb counting down the seconds to zero.

She lay on the bed for a long time, letting the questions pile up in her head. It felt like all the answers to her entire life lay just out of her reach. She pulled herself from the bed and stumbled on shaky legs down the stairs, where she made a beeline to Blake's office. She moved to his desk and ripped open a drawer, shuffling through papers until she found his bank statements.

She scanned the rows of entries, not finding much to go on. But then she found a statement from several months ago with a one-thousand-dollar cash withdrawal every Thursday. She checked older statements to find the same pattern.

All the answers to all the questions of her life came crashing down on her. She knew she should feel rage at such an enormous betrayal, but she felt nothing. She sat before the evidence feeling empty—a hollow vessel needing to be filled but having nothing to fill it.

HALLE led Jet and Shelby through the living room and onto the patio. Blake stood at the railing to the deck, holding an ice pack to his face and sipping Scotch from a cocktail glass while staring at the Golden Gate Bridge.

Halle floated to her father, carrying the framed painting. "Daddy."

"I thought I made it clear I didn't want to be disturbed."

Halle halted, several feet from him. She retreated a step and glanced at Jet, searching for courage. "I know, Daddy, but Pearl made lunch, and I wanted to give you your birthday present before everything gets any crazier around here."

"Tell Pearl I'm not hungry." When she did not respond, Blake turned to stare at his daughter. She stood frozen, not knowing what to do. His features softened. "Wait a minute. What's that you're holding?"

"It's your birthday present." She cautiously stepped forward, holding the painting well in front of her. "It's a portrait of me that Jet painted."

Blake took the painting and held it so the light showed it best. "It's beautiful. He captured your passionate spirit perfectly." He studied the detail for a moment. "Why, Jet, this is fantastic. I had no idea you were so talented. I'm going to hang this in my office so I can see it every day."

"Thanks, Mr. Reardon. Halle's an easy subject."

Blake let out a chuff of laughter. "Halle has never been easy with anything. She was a difficult baby, a problematic child. She got in a fistfight with a boy on her first day of school, and it went downhill from there. She is the most rebellious, passionate, uninhabited spirit I know, and I wouldn't change a single thing about her for all the rice in China. I just wish Campbell were more like her." Blake leaned close and kissed Halle on her forehead. "Thank you, sweetheart. I will cherish this."

Halle hugged her father for the first time that she could remember. "Come inside and eat something, and stop worrying about Campbell. They love each other. I only wish Sayen were that much in love with me, instead."

Blake hugged her back, squeezing her tight. "Oh, sweetheart, you just said a mouthful."

CHAPTER TWELVE

LEADING Shelby between them, Halle and Jet shuffled along the sand, making a beeline for her brother's blanket. *They are lovely together*, she thought, as Sayen and Campbell came into view. The closer Halle came to Sayen, the more nervous energy she felt surging through her. "This idea sucks," she said to Jet. "You'll drool all over him and make a fool of yourself."

"Excuse me; can we tone down the attitude? I'm not trying to steal your dream boy. I just want to see what kind of man twirls Campbell's skirt."

"Like, now that you know he's not into white bread, you think you stand a chance?"

Jet shook his head. "Hardly. You know salt and pepper are the spices I crave."

Halle and Jet plopped down at the edge of Campbell's blanket. Sayen sat up and pulled Shelby onto his lap. They began to play a game of clapping their hands. Halle noticed how the drops of moisture glistened within the hair on Sayen's chest. She also noticed that his underarms were shaved smooth, like Rachid's had been. The first time she'd seen Rachid naked he had told her this was a custom in some Muslim cultures for men to shave their underarm and pubic hairs. Like circumcision, it had to do with some form of cleanliness the Prophet had prescribed. She glared at Sayen's crotch, wondering if his private parts were as hairless as Rachid's had been. It was what she had found most erotic about her ex-boyfriend, that purely masculine body equipped with what looked like adolescent sexual organs. Right then she would have given anything to be able to pull Sayen's shorts down, take his member in her hands, and stroke its loveliness from smooth balls to helmet-shaped head until it reared up unsupported over his belly.

Sayen glanced at Halle over the child's head with a gaze that made her feel at once invisible and seen through. The surprise of it made her suck in her breath, rewarding her with his scent—a masculine, mature aroma.

"Mom is in her superbitch mood, and I blame you two. We came out here to get away from her." She glanced back at Sayen, looking so natural holding the child. She could see his adoration for children radiating from him, and it made her stomach do a slow somersault. "This is Jet," she said, finding her voice again. "No doubt you've heard about him from Pearl."

Sayen and Jet exchanged nods, and Sayen asked, "And who is this little princess?"

"Shelby," Jet said, his voice sounding shy. "My niece."

"Mom needs everyone around her to march to her drumbeat," Campbell said to his sister, "so she can feel needed. She's upset that I'm marching out of step, but that won't last long."

"Easy for you to say," Halle barked. "You explode this neutron bomb, and then fly off to Thailand while I'm stuck in the fallout."

Campbell laughed. "Yeah. Your renegade, fuck-everything attitude must be rubbing off on me."

Halle flipped him the bird at the same time Jet held up a joint. "Hey, do you guys party?"

"Sure," Sayen said. "Fire up that puppy."

"None for me," Campbell said, "and Halle is too far along."

"Hey, Cam, would you take Shelby to the water to play." Halle knew Shelby had seen people passing a joint before, but she would rather not have it getting back to Pearl that it happened with her there.

Campbell leaped up and snatched Shelby from Sayen's lap, throwing her over his shoulder. Shelby squealed as Campbell ran for the surf.

Halle dug through the picnic hamper, pulled out a sandwich, and nibbled a corner. "Sayen, I was wondering, could you teach me how Muslims do that prayer thing?"

Jet fired up the joint, took a hit, and passed it to Sayen. Jet unbuttoned his shirt and spread it open to let the sun touch his skin, or was he flirting? Halle cocked her head, studying Jet's sparrowlike chest and concaved stomach. He seemed a child next to Sayen's virile musculature.

Sayen inhaled twice and passed it back. "Sure I can teach you, but why?"

"The baby's father is from Morocco. On the slim chance I keep the baby, I feel I should teach him something about his father's religion. I've researched some things online, of course, and I've read a biography of the Prophet, and I'm working my way through a translation of the *Koran*." She rolled her eyes to the heavens, trying to remember the exact words. "*La ilaha illallah wa Muhammadan rasulullah*"—There is no God but God, and Muhammad is the Messenger of God.

Sayen smiled. "Sounds like you've put a lot of thought into keeping this child."

She felt herself blushing. "Am I so transparent?"

He hesitated. "Okay, little sister, I usually pray at sunset. We can hook up then, and I'll step you through it."

On impulse, Halle reached out and took his hand in hers. They stared into each other's eyes for a moment, and she felt her stomach rotating again, only this time she felt an overpowering heat along with it. She finally released his hand and took another bite of her sandwich.

They sat in silence until Jet pointed to the water. "Look at them play."

Halle and Sayen both turned to watch Campbell, up to his knees in the surf, lifting Shelby above an oncoming wave.

"One of these days he'll be an awesome father," Sayen said. "I'm sure of it."

Jet said, "Halle tells me you offered to raise her baby."

"Jet!" Halle screamed, spraying a mouthful of tuna fish over him.

Sayen shook his head. "No way I said that." He took the joint from Jet, inhaled, and passed it back.

Jet shrugged. "I thought you figured it would be just the ticket to ensnare Campbell. He would do anything to have a family."

Halle watched Sayen go as still as a mannequin, and she could almost see the wheels in his head turning as he stared at Campbell and Shelby frolicking at the water's edge.

"So like, you guys are honeymooning in Thailand?" Jet asked. "That's so freakin' cool. Wish I could go too."

"Whoa!" Halle said. "Wouldn't that be cozy?"

Jet grabbed a handful of sand and sprayed it over her bare legs. "Dude, shut your chops if you're going to be crude."

The joint made another round. Jet pinched off the burning end and stuffed the roach in his shirt pocket.

"It's off-season," Sayen said, "so there's no problem with getting plane tickets or hotel rooms. You two could meet us there."

"Yeah, like maybe if I win the lottery," Halle said.

Campbell ran up, dumped Shelby onto Sayen's lap, and plopped down beside Halle. He pulled an apple from the hamper and handed it to Shelby, who attacked it."

"Have you thought of a name for the baby?" Sayen asked Halle.

She shook her head. "Mom says I shouldn't name it because I'd get too attached to it."

"How could you not be attached to it?" Sayen asked. "You're feeding it your soul. There's nothing more beautiful in life. You can't ignore that."

Halle felt her being empty of any kind of expression. Her hand raised on its own to caress her cheek as she suddenly felt beautiful. She glanced up to see affection mirrored in Sayen's face. "Why is it that you are the only one who gets that, who gets how I feel? Is that a gay thing? Or do you just love children that much?"

Sayen kissed the top of Shelby's head. "It's not a gay thing." He placed his hand on her belly. "He's kicking. Wow, you should name him Beckham."

"We don't even know if it's a boy," Campbell said.

Campbell placed his hand beside Sayen's. It moved slightly, and they interlaced their fingers. "You're right. *She* just kicked a field goal."

"You can't name it anything," Halle said, "unless, of course, you're planning to be its double daddies."

Campbell held up his hands like a traffic cop stopping traffic. "Whoa. Where did that come from? No way we're ready for that?"

Sayen clutched a handful of sand and let it sift through his fingers. "When will we be?"

Campbell studied him for a moment, as if trying to decide whether to tell the truth or make a joke of it. "When you commit to me for life, so that I won't be stuck raising a child by myself."

Sayen seemed as shocked as Halle felt that Campbell had not only opted for truth, but had revealed something so personal in front of her and Jet.

Sayen lifted Shelby off his lap, set her on the blanket beside Halle, and crawled onto his knees, as if he were about to pray. "Dearly beloved, we are gathered here today in the eyes of God to witness Sayen Hommet taking Campbell Reardon to be his awfully wedded husband for ever and ever, or at least until Beckham has grown into manhood."

For a moment, Halle thought that her brother would lean into Sayen and kiss him, sealing the bargain. That's certainly what she would have done. But Campbell only sat staring, as if not believing. He finally said, "Okay, smartass. I'll think about it."

An awkward moment passed before Campbell did lean forward. They kissed, and held it for a long time. Halle had never seen two people exchange so much emotion by simply touching lips. She felt her eyes tear up, and more than anything she wanted to be kissed like that, like she was the most cherished thing on earth.

Shelby demanded to be kissed too. Sayen pulled her back onto his lap, and even though her face was smeared with juice from the apple, he planted a big sloppy kiss on her cheek. She squealed and tried to break away, but he held her and would not stop. They horsed around for another minute before he set her down beside Halle once more. She took another bite of apple and grinned while chewing.

Sayen stroked Campbell's shoulder. "I see visions of you teaching Beckham how to catch a pass."

"And what would you teach *her*?" Campbell asked.

"I'd teach *him* to call you daddy."

Jet barked a nervous chuckle. "You can teach me that any time."

Jet and Sayen traded lewd laughter and slapped hands in a high-five.

Halle noticed Jet slipping his hand into his jean's pocket and nudging the lump in his crotch, trying to make it less conspicuous. Sayen noticed it too. He exhaled a good-natured breath of amusement.

She frowned. "Yuck! I'm leaving."

Jet leaped up to help her stand. He pulled Shelby off the blanket, and they wandered up the beach. They stopped, and Halle turned to remind Sayen of his promise to teach her about how Muslims pray. When he nodded, she marched away, feeling light and happy again. They made slow progress, but it felt glorious to be out in the sea breeze on such a beautiful day, and excitement rushed through her from the expectation of being with Sayen at sunset.

She glanced over at Jet and saw a self-satisfied smirk. He had flirted with Sayen, and now he was reveling in it. Her spirits suddenly sank. "We were having a perfectly fine conversation until you spoiled it with that lame wisecrack."

"What?"

"Just because you want to jump his bones doesn't mean you can be so crude, especially in front of children."

"Jesus, Halle, could you be any more insecure? I'm not trying to steal your heartthrob. I was only being friendly."

"How can I know if they're serious about raising Beckham if you keep horning in? You twist things around and make a joke out of everything."

"So it's my fault you can't come out and say, 'Raise my baby, you gorgeous stud, and let's make twenty more.'"

"Shut up!"

"I mean, what the fuck!" Jet's voice rose to a shout. "You always want someone else to shoulder your problems, because you don't have the spine to go after what you want. You push your insecurities onto me and then punish me for putting up with your bullshit. You criticize me so you don't have to blame yourself."

They walked a few more paces in silence while anger flashed through Halle. But she somehow knew he was right, and that she had overreacted.

"Whoa, that sounded really deep," she said. "Could you, like, repeat that?"

They both stared at each other and burst out laughing, nervously at first, then assertively.

THE breeze had stilled, and heat rose from the sand as well as fell heavily from the sky. Sayen lifted a bottle of water from the picnic hamper and twisted off the cap. It was still cold, and when he swallowed a mouthful, it chilled his chest all the way to his belly. He lay on his side, leaning on one elbow, and feeling the heat from the sand radiating through the blanket to mix with the coldness hitting his stomach. He watched Halle and Jet lead the child away, and when they were nearly out of sight, he focused his attention back on his lover.

Campbell lay on his back with an arm flung over his face, hiding his eyes in the crook of his elbow; his expression was complicated, unreadable. The afternoon light fell over that alabaster-white skin, which was framed against the blanket and gleamed with suntan oil. A silver chain around his neck highlighted his pure skin tones, and it also glittered in the sunlight. Only that soft pouch covered by Campbell's Speedo didn't glow.

Sayen took another swallow. He thought about the possibility of raising a child with this man, and Campbell's implied promise to make that happen. The picture of them holding a son between them rattled around his head, growing in strength and clarity, until it began to mingle with an image of them making love. Yes, he realized, making love to this beautiful man, as the father of his child, was the sexiest thing he had ever imagined.

Campbell breathed deeply, pushing his chest up and down, working the muscles of his abdomen.

Sayen leaned closer, inhaling the spent breath, which smelled faintly of lavender. Sayen became absorbed in the warm, intoxicating sweetness of this man. The sound of Campbell's breathing mingled with the whisper of wind and the thumping waves. Sayen stared at the length of him, studying each exquisite detail. The paler skin of those soft areas around the green, three-knuckle pouch made his heart race. He took another pull from the bottle.

Sayen's own sex became engorged, curving toward his bellybutton. He wanted more than anything to nuzzle his face to that bulge of Speedo. He imagined himself sucking his lover right there on the beach, bringing them both to a climax, but decided a cold dip in the ocean was the best way to cool his emotions. He couldn't pull himself away, however. He leaned closer and touched his lips to his lover's crotch. The incredible softness consumed him.

Campbell lifted his arm and raised his head. He moved his hand to Sayen's face, caressing his cheek as though he were reading Braille. His voice became a whisper. "You shouldn't have led Jet on. That was humiliating."

Sayen's sexy spell was broken. He pulled away from Campbell's touch and scrutinized the sea, immense, gathering strength, raging against the beach, retreating to regroup and gather again.

When he spoke, his voice sounded far more bitter than he had intended. "You're the one he's in lust with. He couldn't tear his eyes away from your Speedo. Talk about embarrassing."

"Look, Hom, I know you like to flirt, and much as that kills me I can overlook it. But Jet is almost family."

"If you were the father of our child, I wouldn't feel the need to flirt. I'd be perfectly happy staying home to help daddy change Beckham's diapers." Sayen felt a rush of shame as he realized he was trying to bribe his lover into giving him what he now craved. It seemed a bizarre place to have an epiphany, lying almost naked on the beach with hoards of people around, but what rule said that the divine only worked at the mosque and during prayers? As if filled with a sudden flash of light, Sayen fully comprehended that he had, at some point in the last seven months, fallen in love with this gentle man, and that he needed nothing more than to raise a family with him. The realization hit him like a Mack truck.

"Becky's diapers…. You mean that? You'd give up casual sex?"

Sayen stared into Campbell's eyes, and he saw the same level of love and hope gazing back at him. The joy of it almost crushed him. He struggled to keep his voice steady. "I already have. That silly vow was dead serious. As long as I get to take care of daddy, and daddy takes care of Beckham, that's all I need."

Campbell turned away, going utterly still while staring at two kids playing at the water's edge. He was no doubt weighing the promise, gauging how much trust to give this man.

"In two months, you and I could be daddies," Sayen said.

Campbell shook his head.

"Why not? It's your own flesh and blood. We can give your folks a grandchild, and Halle could live with us. She could experience being a mother."

"Jesus, you've really fallen into the deep end, but I love you anyway." He kissed Sayen, a tender brush of lips.

"It'll be an adventure; maybe the most significant one of our lives. And I would get to call you daddy...."

"You know I'd love a child, but—"

"I know how much work it'll be, and it's what I want for us. Please, Cam, don't make me beg like a dog."

"What about Doctors Without Borders? You can't take Becky into the jungle."

"I'll make sacrifices if you will."

Campbell hesitated, and Sayen kissed him, a lingering, needful kiss. Sayen felt his passion rising again. The heat flowing through him felt like a blowtorch.

"Let's make love, right here, under the blanket," Sayen crooned, running his hand along his lover's flank.

Campbell chuckled. "We might as well be in a packed football stadium. But once we get to Thailand, I know a private little beach near a blowhole. Nobody goes there because you have to climb down a cliff wall. It's a tiny inlet with a sand beach, hidden from the road above the cliff. We'll feel like Crusoe and Friday."

"You'll take me there?"

"Sure," Campbell whispered. "We'll skinny-dip at sunset, then make love in the moonlight."

"Nobody has ever done anything like that for me." He put his arm around Campbell's neck, and they kissed. He moved his hand along the muscles of his lover's spine, running over solid waist and back to the wideness of the shoulders. Campbell arched toward him, a white curve of longing. His ribs beat open and closed like a bird's wings, but he remained gentle, touching shyly.

The wind pressed against their bodies like a living force. When Sayen pulled away, Campbell nodded to the outline of his own erection tenting his Speedo. "Now you've gone and done it," he said, hoarsely, softly. "What are we going to do about this?"

The great affection that lay within Sayen, that he had always needed to unchain but never could, rose up in him now like Icarus soaring across the sun. He shot his lover a lewd smile. "Use it to screw me in the backseat of the Bentley."

Campbell's mouth dropped open. Both fear and lust shown on his face. "You're not serious?"

"You want it even more than I do. You give me what I want, and I'll give you what you want. The only question is whether you've got the balls?"

Campbell shook his head. "There is no friggin' way." But at the same time, he had the heavy-lidded, full-pouting-lipped look on his face that he got whenever he needed it bad.

"That's your trouble, Cam. You never do what you want. Trust me."

They kissed again, exulting in the softness of caressing lips.

Campbell said, "It's disgusting how much I love you."

Sayen felt the splendid strength that was locked in his thighs, the weighty power of maleness against his belly, the lightness of his fingertips that had unexpectedly become so sensitive to touch. He stroked the front of Campbell's ridged Speedo.

"Prove it."

Campbell rolled to his feet in one catlike move, took Sayen by the hand, lifted him, and led him toward the house. They entered the yard and crossed to the garage. Inside, the room was hot and muggy and smelled of exhaust. They rushed to the Bentley and flung open the back door.

"Wait. Let's have some mood music," Sayen said, opening the driver's door. The key was still in the ignition. He turned it, flipped on the radio, and turned the nob until he found a '40s music station.

"Dad left the key in the ignition? Jesus, he must have been totally wrecked."

Sayen unfolded out of the front seat, grabbed his lover's erection, and kissed those soft lips. "Get your tush in there and prepare to be wrecked yourself. There will be nothing left but bleached bones."

As Campbell bent over to crawl into the backseat, Sayen ripped his Speedo down. The sight of that porcelain-smooth ass made him gasp. He fumbled with his own drawstring, getting his shorts off, then crawled in and enfolded himself within Campbell's arms.

Music filled the car, Judy Garland singing, "You made me love you / I didn't want to do it / I didn't want to do it...." As the back door closed, their open mouths came together. They wrestled with a competitive aspect to their lovemaking. Sayen instinctively struggled to maneuver on top.

Campbell held Sayen's face with both hands. "Hey lover-boy, you said use my prick to screw you. I'm Leo, you're Kate."

Sayen stared into his lover's eyes, which were mostly pupil, turquoise blue, and blazing with desire. In their depths he saw the edge of something like fear—a trace of vulnerability that belied his insistent tone. Sayen surrendered. "Be gentle. I haven't done this in ten years."

Campbell spit in his hand.

Sayen gasped as the first jolt of pain rode up his spine, but he clamped his jaw shut because he knew this was what he had waited for during the last several months. Waves of sensations, both pain and pleasure, rolled through his core. His mind reached forward to the weeks and years ahead, visualizing being happy with this man, living the dream. This bit of pain was such a small price to pay for such a brilliant future. After all, everything has a price.

In truth, he knew, Campbell had become a superior lover. At first, sex with him had been practical and solid, almost impersonal. There were things Campbell would and would not do, and through their struggle to find passion, there was, foremost, a sense of honesty from Campbell and a determination to make it work. But the pendulum had swung, and now, sexually, Campbell grew open and aggressive and willing and wanting. They moved beyond the complexities of egos, dominance and submission, and became a ballet of enthralled passion. Seemingly amused yet grateful, Campbell taught his lover how to receive pleasure, rather than take it. Sayen paced him—slowing him down—wanting to draw out the experience and give his man the most fulfilling ride of his life. Lying under Campbell, face to face, chests pressed together, each thrust pushed Sayen beyond a new boundary, inching him to a space that became a revelation.

The radio crooned, "You made me love you / And all the time you knew it / And all the time you knew it...."

BLAKE stood at the island in his kitchen holding an icepack to his eyes, while sipping a fresh Scotch. He stared out the window with his good eye, deep in thought.

Pearl busied herself at the sink, pealing a mountain of potatoes. She glanced sideways at him. "Mr. Reardon, what you plan to do about Campbell running off with this boy?"

"I wish the hell I knew, Pearl."

"You ask me, I see all boys Campbell has reeled in, and this one is first keeper."

"Well who the hell asked you?"

Pearl folded her arms over her breasts and shot him a look.

Blake groaned. "I'm sorry, Pearl. I know he's a fine boy, probably better than we deserve. I just wish the hell Campbell wasn't in love with him."

"Be careful what you wish for, Mr. Reardon. Saint Teresa said more tears shed over answered prayers than unanswered ones."

Before Blake could respond, he saw movement in the yard, Campbell and Sayen hurrying toward the garage. Blake zeroed in on the bulge in Campbell's Speedo and understood what was afoot. He gasped for breath, turning into long ragged pants for enough air.

"You feel okay, Mr. Reardon?" Pearl asked.

"Not here!" Blake gasped. "Please, not now."

Minutes later, Blake slipped into the garage and inched toward the Bentley. The car rocked from side to side; the glass was steamed over. He leaned to the window, caught an eyeful, and pulled back.

On the radio, a new song had begun; Jimmy Durante rasped, "I'll be seeing you in all the old familiar places." Blake slumped to his knees, snatched Sayen's shorts, and pressed them to his face, inhaling. He dropped the shorts, clutching both arms around his chest in a protective move. A sharp pain concentrated deep in his left shoulder. Tears streamed down his cheeks as a low heaving sound escaped the Bentley. The car's rocking became more violent. Every instinct told Blake to run away, to put as much distance as possible between him and what was happening in that backseat, but he couldn't. He peered in the window again.

He heard his son's voice saying, "I'm... I'm...."

"Harder," Sayen barked. "Hurt me."

Blake inched away, unable to stand the pain any longer. As he reached the door, he heard Sayen's deep-throated voice, sounding like Greta Garbo, saying, "I'm yours."

Blake tumbled out the door and landed on his knees, while still clutching his chest. It took all his strength to pull himself to his feet and stagger to the house. He needed a stiff shot. He needed several stiff shots.

CHAPTER THIRTEEN

AFTERWARD, sprawled across the Bentley's backseat, they lay in each other's warmth. For the first time, Sayen had found a place he belonged, home, right there pressed to Campbell's chest, his lover's spent breath curling on his neck. He nuzzled closer, matching Campbell's inhales and exhales. The car's interior grew stuffy, and the hair on his torso was sticky with his own semen. Gently, as if not to disturb his lover, he removed Campbell's hand from his ass and tried to slip from underneath his lover's bulk.

"Hey, where do you think you're going?"

Sayen's voice was smoky, his smile tender. "It's almost sunset. I need to clean up and teach our sister how to pray."

"And what if I haven't had enough? What if I want to fuck you again?"

"This from the man who was afraid to let his parents see us kissing? I'm your bitch now, you glutton. Tell me to stay and I will."

Campbell chuckled. "My bitch." He ran his fingers through Sayen's hair. "I like the sound of that. Go teach the mother of our child whatever she needs. Just keep this warm for later." He slapped Sayen's backside.

Before Sayen could move, Campbell added, "And instead of wearing scrubs to the party, let's wear tuxedos. We'll go as grooms."

Campbell had prepared Sayen that his father's birthday celebration would be a costume party, a come-as-you-want-to-be party. They had planned to go as surgeons, but now the want-to-be part had obviously changed, and Sayen could not have been more thrilled. He complained that he didn't own a tux, but Campbell assured him he had an extra in his closet upstairs.

Sayen breathed in a long, even gasp of reverence. The moment had turned numinous, and he didn't want to leave. He kissed his lover again, feeling the full length of Campbell's nakedness against him. This man's honesty, strength, and terror all seemed to touch a part of his soul he only now realized existed. The force of that discovery echoed through all the hollow places in his heart. *I will never be happier than at this moment*, he thought.

He extracted himself from Campbell's arms and from the Bentley, pulled on his shorts, and ambled back to the house, alone, absorbed in the fragrance of memory. He felt invincible. He seemed to have been anointed, touched by the hand of God, and given a glimpse of the divine. He felt that humble wisdom of supreme happiness when all else seems irrelevant.

In this afterglow, he turned his attention to Halle, and was grateful, for he realized that he had not properly said his prayers at the prescribed times for months. Since living with Campbell, his religious devotions had taken a backseat to being with his lover. Being constantly in the presence of an unbeliever had made him shy about performing his devotions. In the mornings after cleaning himself, he still faced Mecca and bowed while mumbling the Arabic phrases, but he was too uncomfortable to roll out his carpet, kneel, and touch his forehead to the floor in submission to Allah. After several months living with Campbell, he had lost the habit. Now, however, he saw an opportunity to return to his devotions as tradition required. He had let himself slip from the community of the faithful, the *umum*, but he would let this girl, this nonbeliever, lead him back to his faith. He would teach her, and together they would rejoin the *umum*.

The instant he entered Campbell's bedroom, he was surrounded by his lover. Campbell's bed stretched into the center of the room, the headboard nestling against the wall in a secure, alluring way. *This is where he lay dreaming.*

Sayen sat on the bed, running a hand over the bedspread, smoothing out the wrinkles he had made. He inhaled the room: the light, the textures, the surfboard propped into a standing position in the corner, the line of framed pictures lining the windowsill.

In one picture, a much younger Campbell stood on the beach with his arm draped over Halle's shoulders, both in bathing suits, both tan, with Campbell's hair streaked by the sun. *They are clearly brother and sister, both pretty in the same way, both glowing with light. Yes,* Sayen thought, *Cam comes from a world of light and easy solutions, and now I'm sharing that life with him.*

Sayen walked to the wardrobe and opened the top drawer, searching for Campbell's smell. It held the warm scent of luxury. He smiled. The minute he closed the drawer, he missed that aroma.

He opened his backpack and pulled out his prayer rug (snuggly rolled and secured with a silk cord) and laid it on the bed. He laid his mother's velvet-wrapped *Koran* beside the rug, and his own paperback copy next to it. He opened his suitcase and removed a pair of trousers and a long-sleeve shirt. He held them up, one in each hand, to ensure they were suitably clean.

A soft knock at the door turned his head as Halle came into the room.

"I have a prayer rug in my room," Halle said. "We can pray in there."

Sayen shook his head. "In Muslim culture, it would not be proper for you to invite me into your bedroom, even for prayers."

"Where then?"

"Some place more public than your bedroom. And I want to thank you for reminding me of my own obligation. I would have skipped this if not for you."

She embraced Sayen, kissing his cheek in a sisterly way. "Let's take our rugs to the beach. The sunset should be stunning, and you won't have to change clothes."

Sayen blinked. *Yes,* he thought, *with everyone watching. Be not ashamed.* He saw the joy on her face, and he couldn't stop from believing that divine intervention was at work. *She wants lessons in being a Muslim, Cam wants a faithful lover, I want to raise a child with Cam.* It all fit together too keenly for mere chance.

"We must both cleanse our hands and feet," he said, "and dress modestly for prayer. Wear something loose fitting that covers your arms and legs. I'll slip into the shower and be ready in five minutes."

She pointed to the books on the bed. "Are those both the *Koran*? Why do you need two?"

"One was my mother's and is in Arabic. The other is an English translation." He picked up the paperback and handed it to her. "I would be honored if you would accept this as a gift from your new brother."

She snatched it from his grasp, staring at it as if it were the key to a treasure chest. She hugged him, and when she pulled away, he noticed a tear caught in her eyelashes. She looked down, tugging at the hem of her blouse. "I'll shower and change and meet you downstairs in five, brother."

He cleaned himself and dressed in clean underwear, long pants, shirt, and sandals, and then gathered his mother's *Koran* and his rug into his backpack before moving to the nightstand to retrieve his wallet and watch. He found his wallet just as he'd left it, but the watch was missing.

He swallowed, staring at that empty space. He told himself that Blake must have taken it back. Of course it was Blake; who else knew he had it or where it came from? He pushed away the panic that had suddenly flushed through his head, and then trooped downstairs to find Halle waiting for him. Freshly scrubbed and with no makeup, she wore a flowing, cream-colored kaftan and held her *Koran* and rug under one arm. She looked pretty with her damp hair tied at the back of her neck.

He nodded his approval. They walked into the yard, crossed the lawn, and ambled to the beach. When they reached the edge of the sand, Sayen saw that Campbell had returned to the blanket they had shared earlier. A feeling of harmony moved through his chest.

He glanced at the horizon. Sunset was still a half hour away, but the clouds already held the kind of light that looks washed in blood, and he was happy there was such a lurid sunset to underscore Halle's first lesson. "I'm no authority on Islamic rituals," he told Halle, "and I'm not the most orthodox Muslim in the herd."

"Not orthodox? You think? Hello, you're gay."

Sayen smiled. "Decent Muslims would censure me for being gay. It's a sin right up there with getting shitfaced and having sex out of wedlock."

She hugged him. "Guess that means we're in the same boat. So let's do this regardless of our polluted souls."

They hugged again. Sayen checked the horizon to ensure it was time. Although the beach was still pleasant, the breeze had picked up. He saw a wall of storm clouds shrouding the ocean, speeding toward shore, but it was still hours away. They could take their time with prayers.

He unrolled his rug facing east. "Lay yours behind mine," he told her.

"No way I'm doing that. I'll pray beside you."

"Halle, this is how it is done in the Muslim culture."

"I am not bowing to Mecca with your ass in my face. In this country, we're equal."

Sayen barked a laugh and shook his head. "Okay, okay, I know when I'm outgunned."

She laid out her carpet where he indicated. Like her kaftan, her rug appeared to be Moroccan, and of inferior quality. Sayen assumed that both had been gifts from the father of her child, and he couldn't help wondering how much this Moroccan had taught her. Would his own coaching contradict what she had already learned? Would that confuse her rather than help? He felt that he was an inadequate teacher, but there was nothing to do but charge ahead and hope she understood.

He talked her through a sequence, demonstrating how to kneel, to prostrate, to glance over the left shoulder, and the right, and when to recite a surah from the holy book.

"What should I chant?" she asked.

"I think the Fatiha is the easiest." He found the pages in her book, and she repeated everything exactly the way he had demonstrated and then recited the surah perfectly.

He stood before his rug, looking to the east. He felt the presence of God within him as soon as he began. The familiar gestures of his body and the sonorous chanting of prayers quickly expanded Sayen's being to encompass all that is. He felt a boundless compassion rise up. It was this part that he always loved most. He was never sure if this compassion was from God or from his own heart, or even, in this holy state, if there was a difference between the two.

A half hour earlier, wrapped in Campbell's arms, he thought that he would never be happier. Now he realized that at this moment, melded with God, he was far more content. The whole of the universe had aligned into a dear perfection, and he felt the radiance of it in every cell.

Through his bliss, he still felt the whisper of wind on his cheek, the day's heat rising from the sand. Along with his own prayers, he heard Halle's voice beside him. The sound of it delighted him. *It is something we share, she and I, we umum, here, together, insignificant in the sight of God, yet precious to Him and to each other.*

When they stood again and rolled up their rugs, he scarcely knew where he was, or who he was for that matter. It had been a particularly moving experience, a depth seldom attained. She was touched as well. He could see it in her face, in her unspoken words.

On the way back to the house, she said, "I feel like I've taken the first step on a million-mile journey."

"In my country you would say, 'You are putting yourself on the path of God.' And I would respond, 'Go happily.'"

They walked across the yard.

"I can't wait to write about this," she said, "about the way I just opened up to the cosmos. I mean, I really felt myself expanding."

Sayen cocked his head as he stared at her. "You're a writer?"

She took a few more steps in silence. "No, not a writer. I mean, I'm not published. I write a blog, like everyone else in the world. I average five hundred hits a day, though, so somebody out there cares what I have to say."

"Text me your URL."

"I'm not sure I want you reading my stuff. I'm not nearly good enough to be published."

In the silence that followed, Sayen heard a formidable, unspoken *yet*.

⌒⫘⌒

CHAPTER FOURTEEN

DRESSED in black tie and tux, Sayen stood in Blake's office, reading a volume of Proust.

The room was large and low-ceilinged, with bookshelves covering the wall opposite the windows. A glove-leather sofa, matching armchairs, mahogany desk, and credenza, all gave the impression of thoughtful affluence, and behind the desk hung a framed, poster-size photograph of Blake shaking hands with Bill Clinton. The camera had caught them in a pose that made them seem about the same age and build, with a strong resemblance. They looked like brothers, two silver-maned lions.

Blake entered the room, still holding an icepack to his cheek. His eyes were shining, and he had a tired, scraggy beauty to him. He lowered the icepack to reveal a face that glowed reddish-purple. His eye was swollen to a slit, making it appear locked into a permanent wink.

"Listen to this," Sayen said. "It's Proust. 'The heartstrings yearn to be plucked at any cost, the soul tires of contentment, the body craves any kind of change, even decimation, even death.'" He held up the book. "Would you mind if I take this to Thailand? I've never read Proust."

The unimpressed look that passed over the older man's face made Sayen wonder if this imposing collection of books had made Blake any more noble or wise or improved in any way. He wondered how many, if any, of these books Blake had actually read.

Could they be merely another piece of the facade of respectability he had so carefully constructed?

Blake walked to Sayen, took the book from the younger man, and placed it back on the shelf. "You let him fuck you? Jesus, you never once let me do that."

Sayen stared at him levelly, not answering, unfazed. He felt somewhat ashamed, because Blake had used that word, which was a perfectly acceptable word, tough and potent and coming straight from life into language, like all the best words; but still in this context it seemed like such a private, intimate word, to be whispered between Campbell and himself, and not a word or an act that was any of Blake's business.

For a time both stood silent, one studying the other, like two chess players taking each other's measure before the game began.

"Cam is the only one, because I know for a fact we are both negative, and because I want to give him everything I have."

Blake turned away.

"Besides, when he screws me, he doesn't try to take anything from me. He fills me with love."

"I want to fill you with my love."

"As usual, you're confusing love with possession."

A silent stare from Blake turned into a scowl. "I've got a bottle of Spanish brandy in my desk. I keep it for special occasions."

"You know I don't drink hard liquor."

"Humor an old man." Blake hunkered by the credenza, drawing out a gold-labeled bottle and two snifters. Sayen noticed that the bottle was unopened.

Blake poured. "I feel so alone, lost, afraid."

"You have to somehow deal with it."

Blake capped the bottle and handed Sayen a snifter. "No, actually, I don't. One word from me about what you're hiding and he'll drop you like that." He snapped his fingers.

"You mean, what we're hiding." Sayen ambled to the fireplace. A dozen framed pictures sat on the mantle. Sayen studied one showing Campbell with hair down to his shoulders, dressed in cap and gown. He took a sip of brandy, which tasted rich, complex, and surprisingly smooth. "Why not put a pistol to his head and blow his brains out. That's the more merciful thing to do."

Blake took a deep swallow, as if to gather his nerve. "You can stop me. Just say you're mine."

Sayen studied the next picture in the row—Campbell dressed in tennis duds, holding a trophy. Sayen turned to stare at Blake. "He'll never speak to you again. It will crush the life out of him to lose us both. Can you really do that?"

Blake knocked his snifter back, polishing off his brandy. He set his glass down, crossed the room, and clutched Sayen by the shoulders, pulling him into a kiss. It was a short, dispassionate kiss, with Blake's eyes locked dead center on Sayen's the whole time. They stared at each other, and Blake kissed him again, longer, more meaningful. Sayen did not pull away—his arms went tight around Blake's waist. The taste of the brandy on Blake's tongue was sweeter than the flavor in his own mouth.

Blake must have seen the emotion in Sayen's eyes because he pulled out of Sayen's grip and walked back to his desk where he had left his snifter. He poured another.

Sayen didn't know what to do. He wanted to comfort the older man, but Blake was threatening to slash Campbell's world apart. He couldn't let that happen, yet if he left Campbell for Blake, that would be equally hurtful. "You've been a selfish bastard all your life, you said as much in the car. So, this once, do something for Cam. Give him the gift that you cherish."

Blake leaned against his desk and knocked back another swallow. "You don't even love him, for God sakes. You're only using him to get my money."

"You're as wrong as you can be, Blake. I know that's the way it started, but things are different now."

Blake shook his head and set his unfinished drink on the desk.

Sayen said, "He's up there getting ready to celebrate your birthday. Can you really stroll in there and break his heart?"

"I will do whatever is necessary to protect him. This is a sad situation for all of us."

"You can't."

"You've pressed me to the wall. It's my only option."

Sayen lifted his glass in a toast. "Bombs away!" He sipped, paused, and slugged back a long swallow that finished the brandy. He felt an unpleasant burn all the way to his stomach where it seemed to detonate in flames."

"Don't make me," Blake pleaded.

Sayen, head down in defeat, set his glass on the mantle and reeled to the doorway, his head suddenly spinning out of control. "You win. Tell him some lie about why I left. That way he won't hate you too. You'll need to help him through this heartbreak."

"Wait!"

Sayen glanced back, shook his head and staggered from the room. He stormed across the living room, gathering speed as he went until he was running for the front door. As he reached for the doorknob, Marilyn stepped into the foyer.

"Sayen," she called, "I'd like a word with you, please."

Sayen glared at her. *What the fuck*, he thought. *Why leave a stone unturned on a day I'm batting a thousand.*

He turned and followed her back across the living room to her office, but before they reached the door, Blake entered the room. He saw what was happening, but rather than try to stop it, he dashed up the stairs.

"Blake, no!" Sayen shouted, but it was too late to stop him. "Shit." There was nothing to do but have his say with Marilyn and then leave for good. Blake had said it himself; it was a sad day for everyone. He walked into her office to find her already sitting behind her desk.

He glanced around the room, checking out an autographed picture of her standing beside George W. Bush.

"You've had quite an effect on every member of my family," Marilyn said. "Even my daughter."

Sayen grinned as he lifted his hands, palms up, as if to say, "Can I help it?"

"That's what I like about you, Sayen, your confidence. It's also what I dislike about you. Your tie needs straightening. Let me." She rose and glided to Sayen. He flinched when she reached for his tie, but he steadied himself. Minuscule particles charged the air. Sayen watched them dance through the narrow space between Marilyn and himself. She leaned closer, only inches away, and Sayen froze, feeling a buzz at his temples where his pulse seemed to throb stronger than normal. He had an overpowering urge to place his palm on her forehead and push her back.

She pulled at Campbell's tie. The black silk reminded Sayen of the silk ropes that he had once used on Blake. He couldn't stop thinking that black silk was the Reardon equivalent to golden handcuffs. Soft and sexy at first, but as one struggled, it tightened, growing thinner until it seemed like wire slicing into the flesh, burning.

"Men and their confidence," she said. "For me it's always been a blessing and a curse. At least your confidence is real, not false bravado. Too many men have that. And of course, I see why you have that effect on my family. You look quite handsome in my son's tuxedo. You clean up rather well, except for those K-Mart shoes. Are they the best you own?"

A warning flag shot up in his mind. "For now."

"I'm not surprised that my son's shoes are too large for you. But as you say, that is a temporary setback. With your ambition, you should grow into his shoes in no time." She tightened his tie a bit too snug. He couldn't swallow.

He leaned away from her and adjusted it. *So*, he thought, *she wants to fight. What have I got to lose now*? "You say it like it's a dirty word. Ambition, Mrs. Reardon, is what people have when they don't have tons of money."

She smoothed out the fabric covering his arm and patted him on one shoulder like a puppy. "My husband has told me about your humble beginnings. Do you find it odd that he knows so much about you?"

"I suppose."

"Why would my husband take such an interest in you? Thrill me with your insights."

"To protect Cam."

A disdainful smile; her voice remained a purr. "Protect Campbell from your ambition, yes. You stand there in my son's clothes and your cheap shoes, the well-scrubbed, hopeful bazaar urchin on the verge of being someone, trying desperately to shed your trailer-trash past." She leaned on her desk, looking perfectly relaxed and in control. "I shudder to think of everything you've had to endure to get this far. All those fumblings in hotel rooms, imagining the day you would be as rich as any of them. The day you would no longer be common."

He instinctively stepped back, glancing at the door. He realized now that he had miscalculated his advantage, and he was locked in battle with a formidable adversary. "I underestimated you, Mrs. Reardon. For the record, I've always been poor, but never common."

"Yes, you're strong and willful, which is not at all common. Forgive me."

Sayen relaxed slightly. Marilyn stepped toward him again, getting uncomfortably close.

"Can I ask about your recent past?" she said.

He shot her a cardboard smile. "Should my lawyer be present?"

"How long ago did my husband give you his watch?"

Sayen felt his smile fade. He saw no open dislike in her face, only a sort of inherent antagonism. They were like two scientists who started with the same initial premise, examined the same test results, but interpreted the data into diametrically opposite conclusions. His mind raced, but he couldn't quite focus on any one thought.

Marilyn broke the spell. "Did you really think you could become one of us? I'm reminded of Dorothy Parker, when asked to use horticulture in a sentence she wrote: you can lead a whore to culture, but you can't make her think."

Sayen slowly closed and opened his eyes, shaking his head.

She held his gaze with a basilisk stare. "Tell me, does he love you?"

"You should ask him that question."

"I'm not sure he needs to know that I know."

"Funny, I would have thought you'd want to know how long it's been going on?"

"His bank statements tell how long, how often, and how much. You're certainly not cheap."

Sayen scanned the room's furnishings and artwork. "Neither are you, Mrs. Reardon."

Marilyn slapped his face, a sharp, stinging blow.

He had seen it coming, the cock of her shoulder, the swinging arm. He could have easily stepped back, but he stood his ground and let her swing away. He paused in the aftermath before saying, "I suppose I owe you that one, but don't ever do it again."

Marilyn stepped behind her desk. She scribbled out a check and dropped it on the desk, making it clear he was not worth the reach. "Take that and leave my house. Never contact my son or my husband again."

She opened a desk drawer and extracted a package of Marlboros and a lighter. She removed a cigarette—the last one—and lit it. She crushed the box and hurled it with force into the trashcan, as if she wanted to punish it for being empty.

Sayen lifted the check and counted the zeros. He whistled softly. "You must be very frightened."

She exhaled a stream of smoke and said almost to herself, "It's the only sure thing you're going to get from us. Everything else is a gamble. Trust me, whenever you think there is nothing more you can lose, there is always something else. Now take that while you can and get out."

Up until now, when he had thought about it, he had been afraid of her. Always before he had made a point of steering clear of American, professional women. They were cold, with no more warmth in them than a brilliant diamond, and there was no pleasure in them. They had sex out of boredom or to bolster their self-esteem rather than desire. And of what Halle had said about her and from what he had seen himself, he suspected Marilyn was a perfect example of that rule.

Yet he toyed with the idea of letting it all blow up, exposing it all to everyone, not as vengeance, or even retribution, but as an expression of himself, of truth, to regain the individuality that she was robbing him of. And he understood suddenly why a man who has lived his life working as a nameless cog for a corporation might commit suicide to express himself, would destroy himself simply to prove his own existence.

"So I walk away and you go back to pretending that your husband loves you? Mrs. Reardon, you deserve more than pretending." He dropped the check on her desk and sauntered to the door.

"I thought you were smarter."

He stopped at the doorway and turned to her. "I'm happy to disappoint you, Mrs. Reardon."

"One word from me, and Campbell will spit in your eye."

"You're too late. Your husband is up there now, telling him everything. I've never seen two more selfish people in all my life."

IN AN upstairs bathroom, Campbell stood in the shower soaping his arms and chest while softly singing to himself, "You made me love you / I didn't want to do it...."

Blake entered, but hesitated while staring through the clear glass partition at his naked son singing manfully under the spray. "Son, I'd like a word with you before our guests arrive."

Campbell jumped back, obviously startled. His hands instinctively covered his crotch. "Fire away, Dad."

Blake sat on the toilet seat, staring at the wall in front of him, not daring to look at that sleek figure only a yard away. "Son, I've been giving your situation some thought, and I want you to know that it's fine by me. You were right, there's no reason to hide it or, for that matter, be ashamed of it. I'm proud of you, son. I always have been, and you've done nothing to change that."

Campbell leaned his head out of the shower, gawping, too shocked to say a word.

Blake could feel the boy's eyes on him. He took a wheezing breath and continued. "So regardless of what happens, or what your mother's reaction may be, I'm behind you a hundred percent." Blake glanced over to see his son smiling.

"I knew you would, Dad, but I didn't expect you to come around so soon."

Blake cleared his throat, feeling something large stuck there, restricting his breathing. "Son, I do have one concern. I don't think Sayen is the right man for you."

Campbell shut off the stream of water and reached for a towel hanging on a rack. "Dad, once you get to know him, you'll love him. I know you will."

Blake let go with a wet, throaty gasp. He covered his eyes with a hand.

"Dad...? Dad, are you okay?"

Blake nodded, still not looking at his son. "How can you be sure he'll make you happy? I mean, he could be hiding dark secrets; everyone does."

Campbell began drying himself. His movements were vigorous, as if to hide some embarrassment.

"Suppose he spends time with other men," Blake said. "How well do you really know him?"

"Dad, I don't care what he's done or what he's hiding. Nothing else matters except being with him."

Blake cleared his throat again. He could not get enough air into his lungs. His breaths were ragged, painful. "There's something I need to tell you, something about him."

Campbell stopped toweling. "Dad, you're crying. Have you been drinking?"

Blake dropped his head, gazing at the floor.

"I love him, Dad. Do you have any idea what that feels like?"

Blake stared at his son for what seemed an eon, trying to reengage his will when all he really wanted to do was surrender. He longed to take his naked son in his arms and comfort that gentle soul, protect that fragile being as best he could, like he had done in the first few years of the boy's life. He pictured that baby, whose laughter used to light up the house. He glanced at the man before him, who still had the ability, it seemed, to light up Blake's heart. "Yes, son, I do. He's intelligent, handsome, charming. I wish you two every happiness. If you want a big wedding, I'll spring for it. Sky's the limit."

Campbell wrapped the towel around his waist and stepped from the shower.

Blake's breaths came easier. "What I came up here to tell you is, seeing you so happy has made me realize that you and your sister mean more to me than anything else in the world. Your joy is what matters most to me."

Campbell reached for his father, drawing him into a hug. Blake felt the joy radiating from his son, or could it have been from the glow in his own chest?

CHAPTER FIFTEEN

SAYEN moved quickly through the Reardon living room, making a beeline for the front door. He felt beaten, crushed. His brilliant future had plummeted from a peak of owning the world to losing everything in the span of an hour. He had no idea where he was going, or what he would do when he got there. He just had to get away. But before he reached the front door, Campbell came bounding down the stairs dressed in black tie and tux.

"Hom, where are you going?"

His lover's voice stopped Sayen cold. In formal clothes, Campbell had never looked so manly or so radiant. He saw the strong resemblance to Blake, and he realized why he had been attracted to Campbell in the first place. He searched Campbell's face for any trace of rage or any sign that Blake had spilled the beans. He found elation. "Did you talk with Blake?"

"Sure did. What a shock."

"I'll bet."

"I think he's secretly in love with you."

"Cam, that's not my fault. I can explain."

"I was joking. He said if we want a wedding, he'll spring for it."

An involuntary laugh burst out of Sayen, surprising them both. Sayen looked down, went silent and still, as if he were afraid that any movement, any sound might shatter the hope rising in his heart.

Campbell sauntered up to him, took Sayen's face in his hands, and kissed him. The soft heat of Campbell's lips consumed him. He felt himself melting.

"What do you think?" Campbell asked.

"I think I underestimated your father."

"No, about the wedding. Will you marry me?"

Sayen kissed Campbell. He poured all his love, all his being, everything he had ever been and everything he would ever be, into that kiss. When he pulled back, he couldn't look his lover in the eyes. He took Campbell's hands and brought them together, as if in prayer. A moment of silence passed.

"I'll take that as a yes." Campbell beamed. "You certainly look handsome. Maybe we should slip back into the Bentley before the guests arrive?"

They kissed again. Sayen gripped Campbell as tight as he could, clinging to him.

"Hey, what's wrong?" Campbell asked.

"You make me happy."

Marilyn entered the living room from her office. "Campbell, I'd like a word with you."

The doorbell rang.

"It will have to wait, Mom," Campbell said as he hurried to the front door.

Marilyn shot Sayen a look of pure loathing before she marched up the stairs.

Campbell opened the front door, and four musicians, a string quartet, paraded in. "You're a bit early, but no matter. You can set up under the awning on the patio. It's right through the living room. Follow me."

As the musicians ambled single file through the house, Sayen pulled Campbell aside. "Can we leave? I mean, could we have a quick drink, wish the old man a happy birthday, and slip off to the airport?" He could feel his hope ballooning. If they could only slip away, perhaps Blake could smooth things over with Marilyn while Campbell and he were in Thailand.

"Great idea," Campbell said. "Take our bags to my car, and once the party's in full swing, we'll slip away."

Sayen hugged him. "You're the best."

"Don't you forget it, either," Campbell said. "Just make sure I'm not only the best, but also the only. I want you to myself."

"You got it, lover man. From now on it's only you and me and Beckham."

BLAKE hurried into his bedroom and closed the door. To his surprise, a small giftwrapped box sat at the edge of the bed. Through the short hallway to the master bath, he saw Marilyn soaking in a tub completely full of steaming water. She had a yellow bath towel wrapped around her head like a turban. Beside the tub lay a bottle of Scotch and an open bottle of prescription pills. She held a tumbler to her lips, sipping.

"My goodness, where did the time go," Blake said in too loud a voice. "We'll need to hurry, dear. Our guests will be arriving any minute."

She simply stared into a void, perfectly still. But a moment later, without looking up, she covered her face with one hand and began to sob.

Blake walked to the bathroom. "Honey, what's wrong?" He checked the level of the bottle and realized that she had consumed an impressive amount for so early in the evening.

She visibly pulled herself together and pointed to the bed. "Happy birthday, darling. I want you to open my present before our guests arrive. It's there on the bed."

"Of course, dear, but why all these tears? It's because you're drinking. It's bad for you to drink so much this early."

"No," she said. "It's good for me."

"Darling, you know better than that."

She sipped her drink, silent as a stone. When he walked back to the bedroom, she set her tumbler on the ledge and stood, then stepped from the tub. She pulled the towel from her head and dried herself, reaching for her Japanese-kimono bathrobe at about the same time Blake reached for the box on the bed.

As he ripped off the ribbon and tore open the fancy paper, she stepped to the window to gaze at the line of red slashed across the horizon. He opened the box and pulled out a watch. His balls instinctively shrunk up closer to his pelvis even before he checked the inscription to verify it was the watch he had given Sayen. With his head hanging, he tossed the watch on the bed and began to unbutton his shirt.

So this is how it ends, he thought, *in the quiet of our bedroom, bickering over her drinking.* He had lost Sayen, and now he would lose her, and without her respectability and her money, he would never have a chance at public office. All he felt was a great tiredness and anger that this was the end of his dreams. What was left of his future, he now had little or no curiosity. For his whole life what lay ahead had obsessed him, but now it meant nothing. It felt strange how easy the future was to ignore when one felt so deeply tired.

Now he would never become governor, and perhaps in time a senator. He would never be able to shape government policy to ensure equality for all people. At least he would not have to fail at trying to fill those enormous shoes. *Maybe I couldn't get elected dogcatcher,* he thought. *Maybe the public would see right through me to the lie at my core. Now I'll never know.*

During a long, fist-clenching silence, he stripped down to his underwear and pulled a dress shirt from his side of the closet.

Marilyn suddenly laughed, a shrill, brutal sound. "All these years I thought it was a younger woman."

The comment felt like a hot knife sliding into Blake's gut. He popped a button off his shirt. It landed on the bed beside the watch. "Dammit!" He ripped off his shirt, flinging it toward the closet, and pulled another from a hanger.

"I know what everyone thinks of me," she said. "Dragon bitch strikes again. But I can't stand by and watch my boy get hurt."

"They'll do fine. Give them a chance."

"When you asked to marry me, after all those men who were so obviously only after my family's money, you already had money, or so you made me believe; I thought, here's a man who is interested in me, loves me. And I allowed myself to fall deeply in love with you."

She turned to face him. "That's why I've never understood, all these years, your passion burning on such a low flame. Now it's perfectly clear. I'm your cover, your badge of respectability. You've put me through lonely hell so that you could hold your head up in society while you did your dirty deeds in dark hotel rooms."

Blake stepped into a pair of white slacks, pulling them waist high. "You were always more than that. I love you. It's just not the kind of love that most couples share."

"How can I be sure that you have any love for me at all?"

Was that true, or had he simply slipped back into the lie that he had made his bread and butter by? He couldn't tell. All he felt was tired. *Love, love, love*, he suddenly thought. *Stop whining on and on about it*. "Love is a shithole, and I'm the pig who wallows in it. Can't you see that?"

"There is no need to be vulgar. Now I can never be sure how you feel about me, or whether you married me for my position and money."

"Fuck your money."

"It never seemed to bother you before now."

Don't go there, he thought. *None of this was her fault, and there's no reason to hurt her even more. It was over before we ever met. How could she know that I meant nothing I said, that all my words of tenderness were coming from a space of pain that needed comforting. Lies were always more successful with her, with all women, who shelter themselves within their own limited realities.*

It was not even that he lied, so much as there was no truth to tell. He had met and loved a man, John Michaels, while serving in the Peace Corps. They had enjoyed an intimate affair, and Blake had felt a profound, consuming love for the first time in his life. He wanted to marry, to spend the rest of his life with John, but his lover was Mormon and refused to come out of the closet. When Blake forced the issue, threatening to expose their relationship to John's family, John hanged himself in a hut in the backwaters of Chile. By the time Blake had met Marilyn, his life felt already over. He had fallen to pieces, and she helped him go on living, enjoying all the best money could buy.

She had introduced him to the very rich, the influential. She had pushed him into a world where he didn't belong and at first despised, that he intended to leave as soon as he had regained his inner strength. He had looked down his nose at all those pompous asses, with their glittering jewels and Cuban cigars, but each day of being what he despised, dulled his ability to leave it, until he had no wish to start over without it. And when Sayen wandered into his sphere, he was able to enjoy the best of both realms.

Now that it had all come to an end, he knew he should not attack her. It wasn't her fault. If it had not been Marilyn, it would have been another. And he knew she truly loved him as a man, as a companion, and as a proud possession. Yes, this rich bitch had become his caretaker, his destroyer. He glanced up at her and saw that she was crying again.

She turned back to the window. No expression crossed her face. She seemed a mannequin except for the tears sliding down her cheeks. "All those times the truth was boldly staring me in the eye. I chose to fabricate ridiculous conclusions rather than face it."

"Yes, I've been unfair," he said. "But there haven't been as many as you might think. Perhaps not as many men as you've had."

She whipped around to face him, and fire blazed in her moist eyes. "You think I wanted those affairs? I was driven to them. I'm a woman; I have needs, desires you wouldn't fulfill. At least I had one way to express myself as a woman, now that chastity belts have been outlawed, now that the stocks and dunking stools are gone."

He was not casting blame. Lord knows he understood about unfulfilled needs. He dropped his head and began to fasten his cufflinks. "I'm merely saying there haven't been many. And since I met Sayen, there's been only him."

Her lips shook, but not her voice. "And you were certainly generous with him."

Blake lifted his head, wondering how much to tell her. Should he tell all, make a clean confession, or try not to hurt her any more than necessary? "Before he left me, my life was not measured by hours but by Thursday nights: last Thursday, next Thursday, and there was the loneliness in between that didn't seem to matter. I would have given him so much more."

"You gave him my son," she snapped. "What could be more than that? No, don't tell me. Be kind enough to spare me those details."

"Their falling in love was pure chance. I never told him my real name, so he didn't know we were related." Now that he said it, it occurred to him that he wasn't convinced of that statement. Sayen could have thumbed through his wallet while he was in the shower. It did seem too monstrous a coincidence.

"Regardless, you're letting that boy run off with the most precious thing we own."

"All we own is a house full of expensive crap. They love each other, and they're good for each other. We can't punish Campbell for my sins."

Marilyn turned back to stare out the window, going grimly silent, no longer crying. Blake looped his arms through his white uniform jacket and began to button it.

"If you had been able to love women, would we have been happy?"

At least she was now talking of happiness and not stuck on love. He had long ago traded happiness for security and comfort, there was no denying that, but she was a good woman, and if he had to share his bed with a female, she was better than most. At least she was rich. She was mostly pleasant, appreciative when they did make love, and she never made a scene. She had been very good to him, and what he had done to her over the years was an act of cruelty.

"If you want a divorce, I'll understand. If not, I'll be happy to continue our marriage," Blake said, but he was only playing out the role, his voice was dead. He twisted the gold ring on his finger, forcing it up to the bump of his knuckle, but not over it. "I can't guarantee, however, that there won't be another Sayen."

Marilyn took her wedding dress from a chest in the closet and spread it over the bed like frosting over a wedding cake. She had intended to go to the party as a blushing bride. "Go ahead, leave me. I don't want to force you into anything. I don't blame you, not one bit. Why would you want to stay? Since I'm not even a woman anymore. You've robbed me of that."

"You're a woman," Blake said, staring at her in that thin kimono. "Take it from me, you're all woman." There was no point in telling her that she was more beautiful now than the first time he saw her in that wedding dress. That was not what she needed at that moment. They had both grown so much older, gone through so many joys and disappointments, the depth of their feelings for each other had grown ever greater, yet it was still not enough. She had yielded graciously to time, and looking back at her then, and comparing that younger woman to the older, more sophisticated woman now, he was deeply moved.

"I'm nothing," she said. "Nobody needs me. There is nowhere in the world I'm really needed."

"You're needed," he said. "Beautiful and intelligent women are needed more than ever."

"Men have said that through the ages, and what they mean is they want women to be their whores, but you don't even want that from me. I'm useless." Her hand moved to cover her mouth. "I nearly gave up on us so many times, but I made myself settle for what little you offered. I'm grateful to Sayen for making me realize that I'm no longer willing to settle for 'happy enough'." She paused, as if realizing she truly was thankful, perhaps for the first time in many years. "But I won't allow Campbell to give himself to a common whore."

He knew her words about Sayen should have angered him, but he had finished putting on his naval uniform, and the weight of it, the heaviness of the pants and the pinch in the shoulders, had worked a change in him, as if he had shed decades, and thereby liberated anxieties and the troubles of his life. Even through the strain of holding in his gut, he felt young, and once again filled with the promise of life in front of him.

A soft knock turned both their heads. Campbell's voice floated into the room from behind the door. "What's keeping you two? The guests are arriving."

"We're on our way, darling," Marilyn said.

"Don't do anything stupid," Blake said. "If this comes out, it will destroy Campbell. If you want to hurt someone, hurt me."

Her back visibly stiffened at the word 'stupid'. She turned to glare at Blake. "This is not about Sayen or you. I will not let Campbell suffer the same heartache that I've had."

It came in a rush, not as a blast of wind or the slam of a door, but as a sudden knowledge at his core that he hated her, had despised her for what she had made him into, what she had robbed him of, or more accurately, what he had given up because of her. He stood there grieving his loses while a burning abhorrence revealed itself in all its fury for the first time.

Blake placed his hat on his head and dropped his arms as if surrendering, but through his hate he mustered up whatever courage he still possessed. "If you say one word to Campbell, I'll drag you into court along with all the photos of the men you've fucked. You might not want to hear all the details, but I'll wager your reading public does."

She gasped, stunned. He saw he had hit the bull's-eye, that soft spot where she was most vulnerable.

"How dare you threaten me! Once my lawyers sink their fangs into you, hell will feel like a fucking resort in the Bahamas."

CHAPTER SIXTEEN

THREE women sat on the couch in the Reardon living room, sipping cosmopolitan cocktails. All three were hefty, big breasted, and had a wattle of fat under their chins. Each one's hair was perfectly groomed, their makeup laid on thick enough to hide moon craters. They each wore a high school cheerleading dress, slightly crumpled now and clinging to their convexities. Of the five men who stood nearby, four wore Cal State college football uniforms, and one wore a Stanford tracksuit. They gathered at the fireplace, drinks in hand, talking in low voices. More people streamed through the front doorway, and Campbell and Sayen were there to greet them. Sayen held Shelby by his side, and she smiled timidly at each newcomer that shook Sayen's hand.

The bright sound of Mozart floated into the living room from the string quartet playing on the patio. Jet, dressed in a waiter's uniform, snaked through the crowd carrying a tray of champagne flutes.

As the last of the guests had arrived, Blake and Marilyn made their entrance, floating down the staircase together, all smiles, a picture-perfect couple. He wore a dress-white, naval commander's uniform, and she her wedding dress, giving the impression of Scarlett and Rhett at Tara, preparing to wed.

At the landing, Marilyn snatched a glass of champagne as Jet passed by. She gulped half her drink as she crossed the room to sit with the ladies on the couch. As she joined the conversation, Mrs.

Hallman was saying to the others, "And did she really run off with a younger man?"

Mrs. Dixon nodded. "Hell yes. I heard he even gave her the clap, but she stayed with him anyway. The only thing that kept her from being an out-and-out whore was she was still married."

"You mean she kept her amateur standing," Marilyn quipped.

Mrs. Hallman threw back her head and snorted. "That's it."

Marilyn glanced at her husband standing across the room, gazing over the room like a great white hunter trying to decide which rhino to shoot at first. She had felt the waves of hate radiating from him upstairs, and by the time it had taken her to don her wedding dress, she knew he was through with her.

But staring at him now, she also knew he had been through with her several times over the last twenty years, but it had never lasted. She was exceedingly wealthy, and the growing popularity of her books was making her even more so. He was addicted to affluence. He would not leave her. There were many things she knew, really knew, like how to write unforgettable stories, and how to carry herself at state functions, and even how to cook a proper soufflé. She could talk books, art, or politics with the best of them. And she knew dead on that Blake would never leave her.

The question she struggled to answer was if she wanted to keep him or toss him aside and find someone who could love her. She had never been a great beauty, but she had never had trouble attracting men. They swarmed around her money like bees to a tulip. So would any other man, even a straight one, come with less baggage? At least Blake had a great tolerance for her affairs, which seemed the nicest thing about him.

Blake had worn that naval uniform to the come-as-you-want-to-be party not because he wanted to be in the military, but because he wanted to be commander in chief. The governorship was merely a stepping-stone, and with his ambition and her money, there was a possibility that one day she could be First Lady.

They had a reputation as a comparatively happily married couple; one of those relationships that occasionally sailed into troubled waters, but always trimmed the sails and found deep water again. Yes, they were much envied at the country club, and that counted for something. At the bottom of all the justifications, the fact was that she did love him, always had. She needed him as much as he needed her. They had a sound basis for a continued union (she couldn't really call it a marriage anymore.)

Mrs. Dixon touched her arm. "My dear, you haven't heard a word I've said. You writers are always off in your fantasy worlds dreaming up new and exciting characters."

Marilyn gave her a warm stare. "Guilty as charged," she said, and allowed herself a satisfied smile.

WITH a look of pure adoration, Jet offered Blake champagne. "Happy birthday, Mr. Reardon."

"Thank you, Jet," Blake said. "Don't you look handsome all dressed up?"

"You really think so, Mr. Reardon?"

"Call me Blake." He patted Jet's shoulder and turned to Campbell. "Son, can you bring me a Scotch?"

A redheaded man standing in the group by the fireplace waved Blake over. "Blake, you old sod. Get over here."

Blake strolled over and shook the redhead's hand. "Glad you could make it, Max. Are you flying solo, or did you bring your pretty wife."

"Naw, the warden's got me on a short leash tonight. She's over there bending Marilyn's ear." Max took Blake's arm and pulled him into the group of men gathered around.

Tom Dixon, whose face already had a boozy glow, shook Blake's hand. "We just met your new son-in-law. Bet that came out of the blue. Listen, this is exactly what we need to swing the gay vote next November. But we'll need to keep the fact that he's a Muslim from the Middle East under wraps. Voters won't understand that angle."

Blake held up his hands. "No politics tonight, boys. Let's just enjoy the party."

"But this is golden," Max said. "It makes you a shoo-in for the nomination. And unless I'm no judge of voters, you'll be our next governor."

"You want to parade my son in front of voters like some trained seal?"

The men in the circle traded confused looks. This was obviously not the Blake Reardon they had thought they knew. "No, no, no," Max said. "We just want him to help your campaign—go door to door in certain neighborhoods."

"Exploit my children for votes?"

His tone silenced everyone in the group. Smiles faded.

Campbell walked up and handed his father a tumbler of Scotch. Blake draped an arm over his son's shoulder. "Of course, if Campbell decides to have a wedding down at city hall a month before the election, who am I to deny him that privilege?"

Every man in the group laughed. Men slapped Blake and Campbell on their backs. Even Campbell let go with a good belly laugh.

HALLE saw Marilyn's jaw clinch as she noticed Halle and Jet standing together on the patio. Marilyn excused herself from the conversation and worked her way through the crowd, stopping briefly here and there to say hello.

Halle posed in her costume, a short white dress that glittered. She had her hair up in a bun, two silk wings attached to her back, and she held a wand. Transformed by the elegant, low-cut dress, Halle was scrubbed clean of makeup. Only the sheen of perspiration covered her forehead. She looked as fresh and pure as rainwater.

Jet's eyes were fixed on her cleavage. "Jesus, Halle. You're like, an angel."

"No, dude. I'm Tinkerbelle."

"Right, a pregnant Tinkerbelle. Trust you to be unique."

"And you look handsome in black tie."

"I look like a waiter."

"Only because you're holding a tray."

Jet smiled to himself, clearly enjoying her attention.

"Most men in tuxedos look like waiters, but you seem more like... a penguin looking for water."

Marilyn strolled up, giving Jet a frosty stare. "Young man, there are guests with empty glasses."

Jet shot Halle a look before slinking off. Mother and daughter appraised one another. Halle's eyes turned hard, defiant.

"You know how I feel about you spending time with him," Marilyn said.

"Sorry if he doesn't measure up to your Republican standards."

"Don't use that tone with me, young lady."

Halle turned away from her mother, looking out over the cliffs and at the fading light of the spent sunset. The sky over the water held the rich color of fuchsia. It was that interval between day and night when time stopped to examine itself. Halle could feel her silk wings moving back and forth in the slight breeze, and she wished they could lift her up and fly her to a distant land. She took a deep breath and turned back to her mother. "I've decided to keep my baby."

Marilyn glared at her daughter with hard, unfathomable eyes until good manners forced Halle to look away. She turned her head to stare into the bank of living-room windows, noting that the party was in full swing.

"We should mingle with our guests and discuss that later—much later!" Marilyn said.

There was venom in her mother's voice, but Halle was not afraid. She arched her back, preparing to fight. Before she could utter another word, however, the three buxom women wearing cheerleading outfits sauntered up to join Marilyn and Halle. Marilyn was suddenly on, smiling, animated, laughing a little too loud. "My daughter was just telling me she wants a breast-enlargement operation. In my day, darling, we used the Mark Eden Bust Developer. Perhaps you could find one online."

Halle glanced at the more-than-ample breasts of these three women and rolled her eyes, thinking the last thing in the world she wanted was to end up looking like any one of these cows. And her mother had better tread carefully, she thought, because just now she was in the mood to tell these old bags exactly what she thought.

The ladies babbled on while Halle glanced inside the living room, which looked beautifully festive with colorful balloons. She watched a woman in her midforties, wearing a wedding dress, corner Sayen. He seemed attentive, and she blatantly flirted with him while pretending to fawn over Shelby. Halle found it amusing that her mother was not the only woman who wanted to be a blushing wife-to-be again. As she scanned the party, she found no less than five brides. Between the brides, the cheerleaders, and the men in football uniforms, she realized that most of the guests of her parents' generation were dressed as someone much younger, as if the zenith of their lives had slipped into the past, and they were left with nothing but a yearning to return to their glorious youth. How sad, she thought.

Halle saw Sayen shoot a look across the room to Campbell. Sayen lifted his arm and pointed to his wrist, where his watch used to be, and he nodded toward the front door. Campbell shook his head, mouthing the words, "Not yet."

Another woman holding an infant joined Sayen. Halle watched intently as he fawned over the baby and then lowered Shelby to the floor and took the baby into his arms, crooning and making faces. Halle turned back to the conversation with her mother in time to hear one of the three women gushing about Marilyn's latest book.

"Yes," Halle said to all three women, "Mother dreams of becoming a female Hemingway: traveler, hunter, adulterer, drunkard, writer. So far she's batting three out of five."

A collective gasp rose from the three cheerleaders as Halle abandoned her mother and glided into the living room, her eyes glued to Sayen holding the infant. She moved around the room, watching Sayen from different angles, seeing for herself what a loving father he would make for her child. Joy, a pure, amazing rush of it seized her.

Mr. Allen took her by the arm. "My dear, you look stunning in that costume. Are you a pixie?"

She shook her head as Jet walked up holding a tray of food. "Hors d'oeuvre?"

"What are they?" Mr. Allen asked.

"Fried wontons."

"What the hell kind of appetizer is that? That's the trouble when you hire an ethnic caterer."

Jet's back stiffened. "I wouldn't talk about your mother like that," he said and walked away.

Halle noticed her father cutting across the room, heading toward her. His eyes were red rimmed with fatigue, which surprised her. Normally he was up for parties, loved being the center of attention. He now, however, moved slowly with tiredness. He took her by the arm and led her away from Mr. Allen.

"Kiddo, you look radiant," Blake said. "I've never seen you so lovely."

"Like you care."

"You couldn't be more wrong. Because it's not simply that you've scrubbed your face and put on a dress. It's because you're glowing. To quote Socrates, 'that day my soul sprouted feathers, took wing.' You're crazy about him, and that's wonderful. Just be careful, kiddo. He can't love you the way you want."

Halle leaned into him and hugged him. "Oh Daddy, he understands me, and he wants to raise my child. Right now, that's enough."

"Yes, you always were the smart one. You deserve to be happy."

Blake kissed Halle's forehead, and she lifted her head and kissed him on the cheek. "I love you, Daddy."

SAYEN, still holding the baby, mingled his way past the four men in football uniforms trying to organize a scrimmage line in the middle of the floor. He made his way to Campbell, who was deep in conversation with Mr. Hallman.

"I think we should open a campaign office right in the Castro," Hallman said, "and you should run it, Campbell."

Sayen leaned close to Campbell's ear. "Let's go."

"Fifteen minutes," Campbell said, not bothering to turn to look at his lover.

The room grew hot. Someone opened the big glass doors to the patio, and the westerly wind circled the room and went out, carrying almost all the party balloons across the decking and down the hill to glide across the length of beach.

Halle sauntered over to Sayen. She wiped some baby dribble from his cheek with her fingers. "You'll make a great father."

Sayen lowered his voice to a whisper. "If I have to leave here, suddenly, and without Cam, would you go with me?"

"Why would you do that?"

Sayen shrugged. "Your mom has turned up the heat, so things could boil over."

She moved closer, their heads almost touching; they might have kissed, but Blake strolled up, took the baby from Sayen, and handed it to Jet. He grabbed Sayen's arm, guiding him to a corner. "You know I love you, that I will do anything to help you. Right now, I think the best thing for everybody is to get Campbell away from here."

"Believe me, I've tried," Sayen said. He looked up to see Marilyn weaving across the room.

"Bastard's drooling over him," she said, loud enough to stop conversation around her. She downed more champagne. Then she raised a fist to her forehead and dropped her head. Her shoulders began to shake, and Sayen realized she was crying. She hurried to her office and closed the door. Sayen relaxed slightly. He knew then that she would not make a scene in front of everyone, but he knew he needed to get Campbell away soon.

Blake caught his son's eye and waved him over. Campbell extracted himself from Mr. Hallman and strolled to his father's side.

"Son, why don't you two slip out now and have yourselves a great vacation."

"Sure, Dad. If you say so."

A wave of relief surged through Sayen as Blake shook his hand and hugged his son. Blake said, "You've made me very happy. I love you both."

Sayen took Campbell's hand and led him across the room heading for the front door, but Marilyn appeared out of nowhere, staggering into the foyer to block their exit.

"You common little tramp," Marilyn slurred. "You're not going anywhere with my son."

Campbell froze. Sayen pulled at his arm, but he wouldn't budge. The room hushed. All heads turned toward Marilyn.

"Twenty feet from a clean getaway," Sayen mumbled. He stared into Marilyn's oval face and perfectly applied makeup, *so perfect that you would expect her to be stupid*, he thought, *but no, she's far from that.*

"Mother, you're drunk," Campbell said.

"Drunk, perhaps. But let's not talk about me. You two are the couple of the hour. How are you two blushing grooms feeling? Or is it brides, I really can't keep track of who's what these days."

Blake appeared in the next heartbeat, taking her arm. "Marilyn, I forbid you to say another word."

"Oh my dear, sweet, devoted husband is here to save the family reputation. No need to worry, dear, I've dropped the whole thing." She pulled her arm out of Blake's grasp. "What is important here is whether our son and his... whatever he is... are happy. You do wish them all the happiness, don't you, Blake? I mean, you being on such intimate terms with both of them."

American women, Sayen thought, *can be the hardest, cruelest, and most predatory animals on the planet. And as they have hardened, their men have softened and become their dogs.* He felt truly sorry for Blake, a good man who deserved better, but then he appreciated that she deserved better too. He felt a wave of gratitude that he was born gay and was strong enough that he never felt the need to live in the closet hiding behind some woman's skirt.

"We're leaving now, Mother," Campbell said. "We can talk about all this when I get back."

"If you're leaving," Marilyn said, "then I'm going with you."

"Don't be absurd," Campbell snapped.

"I've always wanted to see Bangkok. I hear the Thai beaches are spectacular this time of year, and I can be packed in five minutes. You can wait that long to start your honeymoon, can't you, dear?"

"Marilyn," Blake spat, "stop making a fool of yourself. You're embarrassing us all."

"So now I'm an embarrassment?" she said, with a playful lilt to her voice. "I'm only trying to take care of my son, to ensure he is comfortable. How could that possibly be humiliating?"

"You're really enjoying yourself," Sayen said, his voice calm and cold. "A cat with a cornered mouse."

"And why not, it's a party. I didn't come here to be dull."

When she went off to cry, Sayen thought, she seemed a fine woman. She seemed to understand, to realize, that to hurt him she would also destroy Campbell, so the best thing for everyone was to keep her mouth shut. But now she was back, enameled in that American cruelty. They are the damnedest people. Really the damnedest.

"We're leaving now, Mother, and we're not taking you with us."

She shook her head. "No, you're not. I've already told you what would happen if you leave. You can't survive without my support."

Campbell pulled his wallet from his pocket, ripped all his credit cards out, and tossed them at her feet. He also yanked the keys to his Porsche from his coat pocket and tossed them down as well. "Goodbye, Mother."

Marilyn held his eye with a stony glare. "For the last three years, your father has paid your boyfriend a thousand dollars a week to fuck him."

A gasp ricocheted through the room. Even the music stopped.

"That's absurd!" Campbell barked. He glanced at Sayen with pleading eyes.

"Cam, I can explain," Sayen said. "Let's go to your father's office."

Campbell followed Sayen across the hushed room.

SAYEN shut the study door and wrung his hands. "It's complicated."

Campbell knew then that this would be bad. "You've given me seven months of complicated. What I need is two minutes of simple."

"Okay, but remember, however shocking this is, I love you, and I know we can work past this."

Campbell's fear suddenly rose sharply, a cold, hollow fear in all the emptiness where only a few minutes before his confidence had been, and it made him sick. He lifted his hands, palms up, waiting.

"My mother brought me to this country to escape sexual abuse from my brother. She gave up everything for me. We were poor, we were spit at by whites, especially after 9/11. When she lay dying, I gave her my word that I would do whatever it took to succeed, to be respectable. But I had no money, and I could not go back to Libya."

"Can we move to the point?"

"You know I put myself through school with the help of a sugar daddy. What you don't know, and what I didn't know until today, is that he was your father."

Campbell looked around, searching for something to hold on to. He turned his body, and he whipped out and streaked his hard fist against Sayen's mouth. Campbell put everything he had into that punch, but it wasn't quite enough to knock Sayen off his feet. Sayen bent over, holding his jaw. "Dammit, Cam, I didn't know!"

Campbell's head swelled with animal rage. He swung again, knocking his lover's head back. Sayen stepped to the side, lost his balance and fell. He hit his butt on the hard oak floor. His lips were split against his teeth, and one tooth bent sharply inward.

"Get up!" Campbell shouted.

Sayen shambled to his feet. His hands dropped to his side, dangling like dead pigeons. Campbell hit him again, a cold calculated punch in the face. Blood surged from Sayen's mouth and ran down his chin. He tried to lick his lips.

"Fight back, you bastard," Campbell hissed, and hit him again. He heard a crunch and didn't know if it was breaking teeth or a jawbone snapping.

Sayen staggered backward, but braced his feet so he wouldn't fall again. His hands stayed at his sides. "Don't give up yet, Cam," he said thickly through a mouthful of blood. "Get it all out."

Campbell's shoulders sagged with defeat. "You son of a bitch," he hissed. "You dirty son of a bitch." He fell back onto a leather chair and stared at his cut knuckles. He lowered his head nearly to his knees; his hands gripped two fistfuls of his hair. Something in his gut—it felt like a silent scream, much like the fellow in Munch's painting—took all of his self-control to contain.

"Hit me again, damn you," Sayen said, and he swung his own fist in an arch from his side to his face, smacking himself hard and sharp, first with his right, then left, and then right.

Campbell leaped from the chair to grab his lover's arms, preventing any more damage, but he stared into eyes that were wide and full of pain, an agony that mirrored his own sudden distress. The healer in him wanted to wipe the blood away that flowed over Sayen's lips and chin and neck to saturate his white shirtfront, in order to examine the damaged mouth. But his pride refused to let him.

Both anger and pity caught Campbell in the throat, closing his windpipe. His lungs struggled and his eyes watered as he groped in his pocket for his inhaler. He jammed it between clenched teeth and sucked a shallow gasp. A second later he took a deeper swallow of air as the ventricles unwound to allow a smooth inrush of life.

In the now silent room, the sound of music, violins and cello, began the overture to *La Traviata*, the infinitely sad and resigned mourning of struggling lovers. Campbell studied Sayen's broken mouth through the music.

Sayen stood perfectly still, listening too.

Campbell took one more dose from the inhaler before moving to the credenza and drawing out the gold-labeled bottle of Spanish brandy that Blake kept for special occasions. He opened the bottle and splashed three fingers of liquor into a glass. He poured a second glass and carried it to Sayen.

Campbell indicated the brandy with his head. Sayen didn't argue; he opened his bloody mouth and poured the drink down his throat without swallowing. He sighed and stared into his empty glass. Campbell poured him another, but he didn't drink it. He sat on the couch, still staring at the glass. "I swear I gave all that up when I moved in with you."

A drop of blood fell from Sayen's lips into his brandy. He mopped his split lips with the back of his hand.

"Mother was right." *Yes,* he thought, *she had said he wasn't fit to look after himself. He was a fuckup who needed her guidance, even when it came to choosing a boyfriend. How pathetic was that?* Suddenly he hated her even more than he hated Sayen.

"I never lied to you. You never asked how I got my money, and once I knew you loved me, I gave him up."

"You mean once I became your sugar daddy."

"No! It's not like that. We love each other. That's all that matters. We can work through this."

Campbell clasped his hands under his chin, as if praying. He smiled, the satisfied smile of a man who has just figured out the punch line to a joke he heard hours ago. "Love you? I don't even know who the hell you are."

"It was the only way for me to crawl out of the gutter."

"This isn't about selling your body or even about lying. You fucked my father!"

CHAPTER SEVENTEEN

IN HER bedroom, Halle ripped things out of drawers and tossed them into a suitcase lying open on her bed. She was caught in a joyous panic, moving as quickly as she could.

Jet strolled in, leading Shelby by the hand. "Camelot is crumbling, and you're packing for a hasty retreat?"

Halle gave Jet a long, meaningful hug. "How will I get along without you? You could come with us."

"No way I'm getting between you and Mr. Heartthrob. Besides, a new possibility just came available, and I want to see what becomes of it."

"Are you talking about Campbell or my father?"

"Don't ask, don't tell."

She gave him another hug. "Be careful. Curiosity killed the cat."

He kissed her cheek. "Yeah, but satisfaction brought it back. We cats have nine lives."

THE room was silent except for the neighbor's dog barking and the muffled sound of the string quartet. Campbell was on his feet, grinding his fists into his pants pockets while pacing fast in a tight circle.

Sayen felt something inside his chest crack, actually heard it, and the white membrane of his being began to spill out. For a moment, he wished he had never let Campbell seduce him away from Blake. He had reached too far, demanded too much, and now he had lost everything. He wanted desperately to crawl back inside his shell and seal himself in. Most of all, he was furious that Marilyn, of all people, had robbed him of this chance for happiness. Emotions were hitting him furiously: love for Campbell, hate for Marilyn, sorrow for this whole distasteful situation.

"Did he fuck you?" Campbell spat.

"Cam, I'm not giving you a blow by blow."

"I need to know. Did you give him unfettered access to your ass? Or did you just lay back while he drooled over you? Is he good? Better than me?"

Sayen saw the pain building behind his lover's eyes, and he knew he had to say something, to try and ease that hurt. "He was a paycheck, Cam. Nothing more." He felt himself turning even more red from the lie.

"Nothing more? I don't know if that makes it better or worse." Campbell leaned over, looking like he would vomit. He swallowed hard, recovering himself.

Sayen was being as candid as possible, and he hoped that his lover could appreciate that. He felt like he was on some runaway train and was transfixed watching this unreal dialogue flashing past the windows. "Let's get on a plane and work this out on the beach. Just you and me with nobody else there. I know we can move past this. Let me make this better."

Campbell's jaw locked, his eyes blazed. "Get out!"

"Cam, I'm begging you."

Campbell ripped the white monogrammed handkerchief from Sayen's breast pocket. He gave it a meaningful look before stuffing it in his own pocket. He looked like a planet torn from its orbit, left in a void, searching for any gravitational pull.

"We're done! Just go," Campbell whispered.

Sayen felt all his conflicting emotions meld into one—fury. It seemed to blast up from his gut to his head. "You're a coward. You're afraid to face this and work through it."

For a moment, Campbell looked stunned, but then his jaw locked again. "That's my tux, goddammit!" Campbell lunged at Sayen, ripping the coat from his back. In a frenzy, he sprang again and ripped Sayen's shirt away, spraying buttons across the floor. Campbell stood there panting. His back ached with the burden of drawing air. He pulled his inhaler from his pocket and sucked another gulp. He began to choke on it. "I'm fine," he gasped. "Just go."

With a slump to his shoulders, Sayen shuffled to the door.

As Sayen entered the living room, Blake stood at the door saying goodbye to the last of the guests, who were making a hasty exit. Blake shut the door and turned on Marilyn, who sported a drunken smirk. Blake's eyes narrowed. "For a woman who a few hours ago was afraid of gossip, you're about to get exactly what you deserve."

Sayen marched toward the front door. He stopped to boldly stare down Marilyn. "You think you've won, but the reality is, everybody has lost. You especially."

Before she could respond, he marched past her. Blake tried to stop him, but Sayen waved him off.

Halle charged down the staircase dragging a suitcase. "Sayen, wait!"

Sayen halted at the doorway.

"I'm coming with you," Halle said.

Sayen crossed the space between them and took her into his arms, hugging the life out of her. "I'm going to be a father. You hear that? The rest of you can all go to hell."

"You're not going anywhere, young lady."

Halle pulled away from Sayen's embrace. She marched to her mother, cocked her arm, and slapped her mother's face. Sayen grabbed Halle's suitcase. He curled his other arm around her shoulder as she wrapped her arm around his waist. They moved to the door together.

"She's underage," Marilyn barked. "I'll have you arrested."

Those words stopped Sayen and Halle. They stared at each other. Sayen could feel his hatred for Marilyn rising again. She had the power behind her, and her voice was edged with smug arrogance.

Blake let out a painful-sounding gasp. He shot Marilyn a look, shuffled to Halle, and gave her a warm hug. "I've been worried about you for a long time, living in your own world and shutting everyone out. But tonight I watched you get swept off your feet, and even in all this mess, that makes me deliriously happy."

"I'm happy too, Daddy. What should I do?"

"That's the first time you've ever asked for my advice. Follow your heart, kiddo. If you get hurt, then pick yourself up and try again. But if you never fall in love, life is not worth living. I only regret living a lie and not grabbing hold of love when it came around."

Halle hugged her father. Blake turned to Sayen. "Take the Bentley. Leave it at the airport. And you listen to me, you treat my daughter properly and be a good father to my grandchild. Everything I cherish is riding on your shoulders." Blake pulled his wallet from his pocket, extracted a credit card, and handed it to Sayen. "I wish I could go with you, but I just...." His voice trailed off. He paused for a moment before saying, "If you ever need me, Sayen, I'll be here."

Sayen extended his hand, fighting off the urge to hug this beautiful man. When Blake grasped his hand, he placed his left hand over their grip. Blake cleared his throat again before saying, "I would have been proud to have you marry Campbell, proud to call you my son. How I wish things had worked out for you two."

"I was such a fool," Sayen told Blake. "I thought the only thing you had to offer me was money. You're so much more. I love you. I think I always have."

Sayen had never before seen a face express such a profound contentment. It seemed to radiate a thousand different variations on themes of joy, serenity, gratitude—a priceless anthology.

"You showed me my soul today," Blake whispered. "Let me know where you end up."

Blake pulled Sayen into an embrace. They clung to each other, their hearts beating madly, a long and meaningful act of affection. Sayen could feel the older man's warm breath on the side of his neck, then the light graze of his lips along the same spot. Blake's grip all at once tightened and released. When they pulled apart, Blake wiped a tear from his eye.

Sayen took Halle's hand, lifted her suitcase, and they charged out the door.

"YOU can't let her go," Marilyn barked. "She's a child."

The hell I can't, Blake thought. "I'll pack a bag and call for a taxi," he said, as he shuffled to the staircase.

"No! You are not leaving me. I won't allow it." Marilyn seized him, tried to kiss him. He pushed her away. "You walk out that door and my lawyers will make mincemeat of you."

"Bring 'em on." He wanted to add, 'bitch,' but thought he had caused enough pain for one evening. Now he just wanted to crawl into some hole alone and mourn his losses.

"Blake, no!"

Blake unconsciously cupped his heart just as Campbell stormed out of his father's office. Marilyn tried to embrace her son, but he brushed past her. He opened the front door just as Blake crumpled on the stairs. Campbell whirled around and sprinted to his father's side. Blake grabbed his shoulder, gasping for breath.

Campbell checked his pulse, gazed into his eyes. He pulled his cell phone from his pocket and punched 911. "My father's having a heart attack. Send an ambulance to 415 Huntington Drive."

"I never dreamed I'd hurt you, son," Blake wheezed.

"Don't talk. Save your strength."

Marilyn rushed over. "I'll get him a blanket."

"You've done enough already," Campbell spat.

Marilyn's jaw clinched, but rather than defend herself, she staggered to the patio.

As if to affirm his words, a faint siren sounded in the distance.

The siren grew loud out front and stopped in midsqueal. Seconds later, paramedics rushed through the front doorway. They lifted Blake onto a stretcher. He tried to fight them off with arms that had forgotten how. His sophistication and dignity prevented him from raising his voice or using force to resist. He finally sank into their safekeeping as he had done all his life; trapped by privilege. They strapped him down and wheeled him to the ambulance and pushed him in. Campbell crawled in beside his father before the ambulance roared away, siren blaring.

ON THE patio, Marilyn sat in a lounge chair staring out over the black Pacific. She held a tumbler of Scotch, taking deep gulps. The clouds that had been marching to shore all day had now blotted out the stars. A light rain began, but Marilyn made no move to protect herself from the weather. She remained seated, letting the water gather on her face, her body. She had no strength to defend herself.

Pearl shuffled across the patio and stood beside Marilyn. "Dinner is ready, Mrs. Reardon. Shall I bring you a plate or would you prefer to eat at the table?"

"Just put everything away and lock up."

Pearl reached out and took Marilyn's quivering, manicured, ring-laden hand in hers. Was that just to touch her, or to steady her? Whichever, she welcomed the gentle contact. She felt an emptiness so profound that she grasped the true nature of empty; it is not merely when there is a void inside, but rather, when the container is broken and will never hold anything again, ever.

"Mrs. Reardon, what's going to happen now?"

"I don't know, Pearl. I just don't know." Unspeakable loneliness and self-pity, both blind and mute, rose up in her, trying to bring tears that wouldn't come.

It had grown so dark that she could see the hand of light passing over the dark waters from the lighthouse at the Marin Headlands. In the gloom below the cliff, the continual detonations of surf grew loud. And then, as she often did when it was getting dark and she had drunk too much, she began to think about what improvements and additions she would one day make to the house and garden.

CHAPTER EIGHTEEN

SAYEN sat in seat 34B, with his mouth torn and his teeth broken. As a kind of penance, he had not washed his face or made any attempt to administer first aid to his mouth.

The whole time he had sat in the terminal, and also on the plane before takeoff, he held his phone in his palm, waiting for the call. Many times during that wait he had thought about calling Campbell and leaving a message, but he couldn't muster the courage. He wanted badly to run his fingertips over that amazing physique and take that beautiful cock inside his own body. He craved to hear Campbell gasp as he rose into orgasm, and smell the aroma of his lover's cum around him while being pulled into a sleeping embrace. But the call never came. He had lost his lover, his love, their chance at being a family, and even though he had brought it on himself, he felt victimized. It seemed like a sudden and brutal trouncing that demolished his self-respect. He moved in slow motion, aware of the pain, conscious that everyone else was staring, judging. Above all he felt the loss, a forfeiture of something cherished that was unrecoverable.

As the plane banked to turn west and voyage over the vast stretch of water between continents, Sayen saw massive thunderclouds building, the city light reflecting off the mounds of black vapor. Below, he could still make out the grid of white-and-yellow dots. The marks of man seemed frail on the plain beneath the billowing clouds, and then he could only see blackness.

Sayen stared into the night. Halle rested her head on his shoulder, already asleep. The blackness outside the window seemed to fade, and Sayen saw, so very clearly, himself sitting in Campbell's apartment that very first time, sipping expensive wine, wanting so desperately to make love with Campbell but having to hold back, until Campbell started to unbutton his shirt. Then he felt himself surrender, that wonderfully exhilarating feeling of reaching for everything he had ever dreamed of—not the brass ring, but the golden ring—and having it reach back and take him wholly, knowing that he had been judged and found acceptable by the pinnacle of his aspirations.

The scene switched to them driving along the coast highway in Campbell's Porsche, and that kiss, so consuming, so full of promise. Watching that picture now, he saw that he had been already deeply in love with Campbell at that point, but didn't yet know it. He not only saw it while sitting in his coach seat, he felt the love flowing up through his chest and being exchanged in that touching of lips.

The scene switched again to the lovers playing basketball in the Reardon driveway. Even though Sayen was the stronger athlete, Campbell was the more skilled player. It had been exciting to test his physical skills against Campbell, and he realized that this rivalry extended off the court as well. And that physical rivalry now showed itself as the boys on the beach, wrestling like lion cubs. Yes, with Campbell he could, at times, be lured back into boyhood and experience the joy of youth, playful life literally bursting from his being. It was the one advantage Campbell had over Blake, and why Sayen had fallen so much more deeply in love with the son over the father.

The vision mutated into them in the back of the Bentley, surrounded by such affluent luxury, making love both tenderly and fiercely. He relived that feeling of giving everything one possessed, and being consumed until there was nothing left to give or take. And after, lying in a warm embrace, knowing that nothing, ever again, could bring such a feeling of contentment. It was a moment of enlightenment, that joining with the divine light.

Sayen slammed the window shade down and turned off the overhead lamp.

Eyes closed, a tune began to repeat in his head, and he hummed along, with starts and stops until a song began to emerge. He remembered only bits and pieces of the lyrics: "flows of angel hair" and "ice cream castles in the air" and something about "feathered canyons." He repeated the simple tune over and over until it became recognizable. As he remembered the words, he began to sing softly, giving each phrase a full measure of emotion— deep emotion. He sang an unhurried interpretation of Joni Mitchell's "Both Sides Now," finishing with:

It's life's illusions I recall

I really don't know life at all.

CHAPTER NINETEEN

BLAKE'S eyes fluttered open. Minutes passed as he fully regained consciousness. He could not remember who he was. Everything felt alien, as if the familiar parts of him had disintegrated and the rest were dissolving. He lay suspended in a vacuous inner space, a sphere of unbroken silence, peeking out at an unfamiliar world with an unblinking stare.

Fear pinched his vagus nerve. A sickly shrinking away from whatever crouched in front of him, dead ahead. But then his cortex slipped into gear and began to explore the state of his strange universe: toes wiggled, legs stretched, back arched, fingers curled into a fist. His entire body clenched and relaxed. He began to study the world outside his body.

Gray light bled through windows. The sun, a blurry spot of weak yellow, edged between the horizon and a thick cloud cover, gave him enough light to realize that he lay in a hospital room.

The top half of his bed was tilted upward at a twenty-degree angle, giving him a view of tile walls, a television hanging from the ceiling, a bed-table—all sterile and dreamlike. The air had an antiseptic stench, reminiscent of cheap grappa, and so strong he seemed to ingest it rather than inhale it. Two beds filled the tiny room, with curtains that could separate one bed from the other.

The bed against the far wall was occupied by a sleeping man huddled in a fetal position with one arm dangling over the side of his bed. The man was clearly a decade older than Blake, and seemed to have trouble breathing, even in sleep.

In that tiny room, the beds were so close together that if he leaned over the rail and stretched, he could touch the hand of the sleeping man. He felt somewhat sheltered by the room's smallness, and with the closeness of that sleeping body there was hardly any room to feel alone.

Nevertheless....

A tube snaked under Blake's nose, spraying oxygen up his nostrils, and a flurry of wires attached to electrodes were stuck to his skin with flesh-colored tape, feeding impulses to a bank of monitors that stood beside his bed, recording his heartbeat, brain activity, blood pressure. He felt like a butterfly pinned to a spreading board.

He had vague memories of waking in a different room— intense lights, beeping machines, that same grappa stench, white coats with human heads wearing green masks all bobbing around. It must have been the intensive care unit, but he couldn't be sure. The white coats would appear like apparitions, surround him, prod him, ask questions he couldn't answer, and vanish. He wasn't sure if they were real.

He heard muffled sounds. As he shifted his head, shapes came into focus. On the other side of an open doorway, a young man debated with a woman dressed in a lab coat covering her green scrubs. An ID tag hung from her front pocket. Her back was straight, shoulders delicate. She held up an X-ray sheet and pointed to a spot as they both studied it.

She held up another. Blake was touched by how vulnerable the young man appeared. His face grew pale and translucent. It mirrored the white blurs on the black X-ray sheets. Then recognition kicked in, and he knew the young man was his son, Campbell. And with that recognition came all of Blake's memories, his personal history, pressing on Blake's chest like a boulder. He struggled to suck air into his lungs as regret washed over him.

He heard his son's voice. He couldn't make out the words, yet he knew that tone; he knew all of his son's voices. That tone meant that Campbell was terrified. He watched the woman shake his hand as her face molded into an expression of hope. Then she walked way.

Pain began to grow through the inside of Blake's head, blinding him. His brain tissue sizzled. He closed his eyes against the pain, and a few moments later felt something squeeze his hand. Opening his eyes, he watched Campbell sit on the side of his bed. He wore jeans, a polo shirt, a black-and-orange Giants ball cap, and a wounded smile. His face now seemed shrunken, as if all the joy in him had bled out, deflating him. Sitting there in the almost polar bleakness of this setting, he seemed lost.

Blake shifted his head, and realized that his headache had grown monstrous. He tried to ask Campbell what happened, but he only managed a groan.

Campbell leaned forward and held his father while he placed another pillow behind his head. Campbell's unshaven face burned Blake's cheek.

"Hey, Dad," Campbell said. "I hope you feel better than you look."

"How long...." Blake's voice trailed off before he could finish his question.

"Overnight in Intensive Care; they moved you here a few hours ago." His chin trembled. He buried his face in Blake's shoulder and hugged him. "Oh God, I was so scared."

"My head hurts like hell."

Campbell smiled that wounded smile again. "You've had a heart attack, but you're going to be fine. You just need to take it easy from now on. No more skydiving."

"Don't bullshit me, I know I'm dying."

"Dad, they performed an angioplasty procedure. The doc says you're strong enough to fight this, and I'm here for you. You'll be fine." Campbell ran his hand through Blake's hair.

"Your mother?"

Snatching a handkerchief from his pocket, Campbell wiped some dribble off his father's chin. "She's in the waiting room. I'll go get her."

Blake shook his head as he felt the need to piss coming on with an urgency.

"I don't want to see her." He was somewhat relieved that Campbell didn't insist. "I need to pee. Help me to the toilet." He began to lift himself, but Campbell pressed a hand to his chest and pushed him back onto the mattress.

"I'll have a nurse bring you a bedpan."

"No. Help me up." Blake could not explain it, even to himself, but it was vitally important for him to pass water on his own terms, standing like a man.

"Dad, you're all wired with electrodes. You can't leave the bed."

Blake reached up and ripped the tape from his chest on one, then another from his temple. The machines beside the bed began to beep.

"If you won't help me, then stand aside. I'll do it myself."

Campbell helped untangle his father from the wires and levered him out of bed, and with one arm about his father's waist, they shambled across the narrow floor to the tiny bathroom. With Campbell for support, Blake pulled the thin cotton blouse aside and began to pee into the bowl.

Blake glanced into the mirror over the tiny sink. Staring back at him was not so much his face, but a manifestation of his predicament. Fifty-nine years of bad decisions expressed in terms of a leaden, harassed stare, sagging cheeks, mouth weighted down at the corners into a grimace, and limp folds of wrinkled throat. The reflection seemed exhausted, a marathon runner who didn't have another mile left in his spent muscles yet can't stop plopping one foot in front of the other. Not out of being heroic, but simply because he couldn't imagine an alternative.

A nurse shuffled in, thin as a pencil, with bright red hair that had to be a bad dye job. She seemed very businesslike, which had a calming effect. Her nametag read, Sara Walker. "I see you're determined to be a problem child."

Blake grumbled, "I'm no child, and I didn't ask to come here."

She laughed. "No, you didn't, but now that you're here, your ass belongs to me. I'm overworked and underpaid, so help me out here."

"Just let me piss without an audience, and I'll be putty in your hands."

She laughed again and asked Blake if he was feeling any unusual pain. He gave her the rundown. She nodded like she knew everything he had to say before he said it. She sauntered over to the beeping machines and turned them off. "If you're out of bed and walking around, I guess we can do without all this." She added that the doctor would see him soon and swished out through the doorway.

As Campbell helped his father back to the bed, Blake glanced at the nightstand that had a sea-blue vase that held roses bursting through a cloud of baby's breath. The roses, tall and proud, were the color of blood and were arranged in a bouquet style. A cream-colored card with handwriting on it leaned against the vase. He squinted to read the print, but it was too far away.

"Those are from mother," Campbell said. "The card says: I'm sorry, darling."

"I'm surprised they're not dragon lilies." As he lifted himself onto the bed, he shifted his head so he stared directly into Campbell's eyes. "I'll tell you something, son. I could die happy if I felt you still loved me. How can a man be content when his flesh and blood despises him? I want you to forgive me."

From the look on his son's face, Blake could see that the boy's insides were churning, and within the myriad emotions marring that beautiful face, he recognized sympathy, slowly rising above the others.

"It's not that I don't love you."

"No," Blake said stubbornly. "Listen to me, son. I got something to say, and I don't have much time left, so shut up and pay attention for once in your life."

Campbell grasped his father's hand and nodded. "Okay, Dad, but take it easy; don't strain yourself; go as slow as you can."

Blake squeezed his hand and held it tightly. The uncharacteristic gesture surprised them both.

"I never dreamed I'd hurt you, son," Blake wheezed. His words came one after the other in a slow, cold procession. "Neither did he. He's fond of me, but he loves you body and soul. Don't throw that away because I was a fool." He took a deep, sorrowful breath.

Campbell reached over and picked a tiny white bloom off the baby's breath. He held it in his hand, as if to measure the weight of it. Then he dropped it on the floor and crushed it with the toe of his shoe, like Blake had seen so many people do with cigarette butts.

It became a strange and sobering moment. He wanted so desperately for his son to understand that all the wounds he inflicted were unintentional, that he wasn't a cruel man, unless weakness was another form of cruelty.

Blake coughed and his head shook violently.

"Dad, you need to stay calm. Be quiet now."

"No," he gasped. "I'm not done yet. You see, my selfishness killed any chance your mother and I had for a marriage, but there's still you and me. We let twenty-five years go by without talking about our both being gay, without trying to open up and understand each other. And that's not all my fault, as you well know. You're more like your mother than you realize. Stubborn and vengeful and too damned wrapped up in your own pride." Another coughing fit racked his body. "We're both in love with the same man, and we need to find a resolution or it will destroy you. I'm trying to meet you halfway. The question is, are you man enough to meet me halfway?"

Blake waited for his son to make an attempt at conciliation, but before Campbell could gather his thoughts, Blake coughed again, a series of heavy, watery coughs that shook his body and left his eyes streaming.

Campbell pressed a hand on his father's chest. "Don't push yourself, Dad. It's time you got some rest." He leaned forward and kissed his father on the forehead.

Blake stared up through watery eyes. He shut his eyelids and his face relaxed.

"You need to build your strength, Dad. You see, if Sayen and I do get back together, it will be to raise Halle's baby. If that happens, and I said *if*, we'll need someone to give us some pointers on raising kids. We'll need help. I'd be proud if it were you, Dad."

Blake's eyelids opened, and he stared at his son. He could feel his face growing stark and strange, small and very frightened. He had a peculiar kind of tightness in his chest, as if he were waiting for the savage blow that would surely come, but he wanted desperately to live so he could help raise his grandchild.

But his hope suddenly died because he could tell by the tone in Campbell's voice that his son was only humoring him. Campbell had no intension of getting back with Sayen. Blake tried to speak, though breathing hard and with effort. "Be a better man than me, son. You and Sayen have something special, and that only comes around once or twice in a lifetime. Don't throw it away." He wanted to say more, but the effort proved too much. He closed his eyes, gasping for air, until he no longer struggled. He lay peacefully, awaiting whatever fate had in store.

Campbell left with a promise to return at lunchtime. The room grew deadly quiet.

The longer Blake lay in that silent room, the more convinced he became that his time was at an end. It wasn't so much that he felt his body shutting down, but more that he couldn't see any future out in front of him. He had lost everything, and life had nothing more to give. He felt ready to give in, to die.

He heard a soft knock at the door, and his eyes fluttered open. Jet stood in the doorway dressed in saggy jeans and a hooded sweatshirt. He held a box of See's candy.

"Mr. Reardon, are you awake?" He stepped into the room, and his smile seemed to sparkle when Blake waved him over to the bed.

"How many times are you going to make me ask that you call me Blake?"

"This will be the last time. I promise."

Jet reached up and took the older man's hand, giving it a tender squeeze. "You had us all so worried. Ma has lit so many candles at church they've shut down the central heating. She says that as soon as you come home she's going to make her roasted crab dish."

Jet did not let go of Blake's hand.

"I'm not sure I'll be coming back home."

"You got to, Mr. Rea—I mean, Blake. I've already told Ma that I'm the one who'll be taking care of you to get you back on your feet."

"I appreciate that, Jet. I do. But...."

Jet laid the box of candy on the bed alongside the older man. "Halle told me you had a sweet tooth, so I brought you some nougat and chocolates."

"Nougat?"

"Halle said it's your favorite."

Blake managed a smile. "Nurse Walker will tan my hide if she sees this. No, no, don't take it away. I want her to walk through the doorway just as I take a big, sugary bite." He laughed at the image of her shocked face. "The next time you come, can you bring me a few cigars? That should really get her goat."

Jet's smile blazed. He bent over at the same time he lifted Blake's hand, gently brushing his lips to the older man's palm.

Blake began to realize that he did indeed have a future to look forward to, new experiences to savor—a roasted crab dinner to celebrate his return, this lovely young man to help him get back on his feet, and the little torments that he held in store for Nurse Walker. Yes, he began to look ahead into that fuzzy void called future, and those blurry shapes grew recognizable. With a bit of a jolt, he realized he wanted to live.

CHAPTER TWENTY

CAMPBELL sat at the counter in his apartment kitchen, waiting for Mr. Coffee to finish brewing the first pot of the day. He shook four Tylenol from a plastic bottle into his palm, and popped all four into his mouth. He began to chew them dry, which had become his latest habit.

He had the blinds drawn so the room was still relatively dim with only a few buttery bands of morning light pouring onto the countertop. He set the bottle down and held his head with both hands, pressing hard in an attempt to lessen the monstrous ache behind his eyes. He heard the sound of his toilet flushing, and a moment later the spray of the shower. The pain in his head grew as he tried to remember their names; Fred and Bob, or was it Frank and Rob? It didn't matter because he had no plans to invite them back. He wanted them gone. In fact, he wanted to erase the entire escapade from his mind, like he had done with so many others.

He glanced at the wall clock, realizing that he had to somehow pull himself together and be at the hospital for rounds in less than an hour.

One of Campbell's overnight guests—the younger one—padded into the kitchen wearing only a pair of surgically-white briefs and a Saint Christopher's medal. Campbell's eyes zeroed in on the cheap-looking medallion and moved down that rippled stomach to his crotch, where an impressive erection strained the cotton shorts. He couldn't have been more than twenty years old, with an angular body, thin face, buzz cut, and rimless glasses.

Campbell seemed to remember it was this one who had worn a somewhat sporty Hawaiian shirt, which contrasted with everyone else at the bar, making it clear that he and his companion were not locals. That's what had attracted Campbell, more than the boy's fresh looks. It was clear they were tourists, just passing through. It was a one-night stand that couldn't develop into anything more.

The boy sauntered across the kitchen, slipped four fingers into the waistband of Campbell's sweatpants, and gave him a dawdling kiss. Those cold fingers began to cool the warmth in Campbell's groin.

"I smell coffee," the boy said with a Midwestern twang.

"Help yourself, Fred, but make it quick. I've got to run."

"I'm Billy, and my friend's name is George."

"Sorry, Billy."

"I'm not sorry at all. You never told me your name. Who are you?"

Campbell's mind spun. *Who am I? Who have I become in the two years since losing Sayen?* He wasn't at all sure. All he knew was that he wanted to hide from Billy's hopeful blue eyes that seemed to stare straight through to his soul.

"Nobody," Campbell said with a lifeless voice.

"Well, Nobody, you were hot last night. I hope we didn't wake your neighbors." He sprung on Campbell like a bear trap, crushing the air out of his chest with a constricting hug.

The pain in Campbell's head leaped into the red zone as details of last night came into focus. Billy's boyfriend, midthirties and unattractive, was an ex-Marine with a considerable toughness. He used the boy as bait to attract Campbell into a three-way. George apparently liked to watch, and seemed quite content to lie there while Campbell rode Billy's ass like a bucking bronco. The harder Campbell slammed into that firm backside, the louder the boy's moans grew until Campbell stuffed Billy's underwear into his mouth to muffle those obnoxious cries. He didn't remember anything after that, but he had a sinking feeling that good old George had fucked him with the same level of violence before lights out.

Billy relaxed his embrace and kissed Campbell again. While his tongue explored Campbell's mouth, he took Campbell's hand and moved it over his crotch. He broke off the kiss and whispered in Campbell's ear, "I could drop George in a heartbeat for you."

The one thing that Campbell could not remember was if he had taken the time to don a condom before fucking this kid. And what about George? Suddenly, his stomach performed a series of cartwheels. He couldn't take a breath of air. He reached for his inhaler and pumped himself a double blast. He could breathe again, but his stomach was still on the verge of retching.

Campbell pushed Billy away. "Forget the coffee; you don't have time. Get your clothes and your boyfriend and leave."

"What the fuck? Who do you think you are? We're real people, you know. You're no better than all those pretentious LA fags."

"Just go."

"You bet we will. Who the hell wants to hang out with a low-class asshole?"

Campbell sat there sipping coffee and listening to the couple's outraged voices while they yanked on their clothes and stomped out the front doorway. Alone again, he grabbed a second cup and hurried to the bathroom. He tried to forget his fear, but he couldn't help wondering how long it had been since his last blood test, or more correctly, was it too soon for his next?

He dropped his pants, sat on the toilet, and let his body begin to purge itself of last night's liquor and this morning's fear.

His iPhone buzzed from the bedroom. *At least they didn't steal my phone*, he thought, remembering it had happened six times since his breakup with Sayen. Because he assumed it was the hospital calling, he jumped up and shuffled into the bedroom, like a man in a sack race.

"This is Dr. Reardon."

"Hello, Campbell. Did I catch you at a bad time?" His mother's voice was flat, with the trace of an apology behind the words. He knew she was blameless that he stood in his bedroom with his sweatpants swaddled around his ankles and a soiled, unwiped ass. On the other hand, he couldn't deny that she was positively clairvoyant about picking the most inopportune moments to call.

"Considering how my morning started, I should have expected it."

"You're sure?"

"What do you want, Mother?"

"I was afraid if I waited any longer you'd be doing rounds. My goodness, I hadn't realized it had gotten so late. Shouldn't you have started already?"

"Mother, I'm late. If you can't come to the point, I'm hanging up."

Silence. He'd offended her, yet again, but he didn't care. It was how he deliberately kept her at a distance to escape her possessiveness.

"Son, are you free for dinner on Christmas Eve?"

"No. Afraid not." He wondered if she could hear the lie in his tone. It was the desperation in her voice that decided it for him. He was in no mood for another of her awkward attempts at making amends. Christmas was still two weeks away, and he had ten days of vacation scheduled from the twenty-second to New Year's Day. He had no plans. The thought sent a chill of anxiety up his spine. He considered flying to Mexico, some place with only a beach and a bar where he could vegetate without drawing a sober breath the entire time. But he knew that would not happen, as he felt himself becoming coldly bored with the idea.

"Oh-I see.... I actually assumed you would be on call that night. I know I should have asked sooner so you could reschedule work, but I've been so busy. I've found you the perfect present. The one thing in the world you need." She sounded stunned. Her voice grew quiet, yet hopeful. "I was counting on you being here. A big surprise. I don't suppose you could rearrange—I mean—I guess it's something terribly important?"

His face puckered into a guilty grimace, but he would not be bullied. "I'm afraid it is, Mother."

"I see. Never mind then. I'm sorry to have kept you. Perhaps we can get together for a quiet dinner before New Year's? I'd really love to give you your present in person."

He grew truly mad at her. "Of course. Give me a call when I'm in my office, and I'll check my calendar."

"I'll do that, son. Goodbye."

IF EATING is regarded as a sacrament, then the Saint Francis Hospital cafeteria was likened to the bleakest Tibetan monastery. The bland fare was neither appetizing nor comforting. The room was too antiseptic with its tiled floors and chromium-and-plastic tables, too chilly, and far too quiet. Most of its patrons were relatively old; Campbell was the youngest person there. He stood with an empty tray in hand, staring at the steaming casseroles and soups and vegetables, feeling glum and defeated. He had no stomach for the food, and even less for the environment. Hospitals are cold and depressing, filled with people on the verge of death. He had lost a patient just hours ago, which had plummeted his already abysmal morning to rock bottom. To feel any worse he would need to pull out a jackhammer and excavate through shale.

He blamed his parents—actually his mother—for forcing him into this dreary profession. He could have become a corporate executive rolling in stock options, or a guitarist playing in a rock band, or a thousand other careers more enriching than working with death. Had he chosen for himself, had he gone a different path, something simple, he could have been a success, perhaps even happy. He could feel the hate for his mother rising for the second time that morning.

He strolled down the serving stations, selecting a fruit bowl and a square of lime-green Jell-O on a yellow plate.

"You on a binge diet, or are you hungover again?"

Campbell looked up to find Porter Cunningham—an angelic vision in a white coat over green scrubs—behind him in line. Campbell shrugged and looked down at his food, thinking he should have made better choices, and then at Porter's plate of goulash and garlic toast. His stomach lurched.

"Jesus, Campbell, lighten up. You're giving depression a bad name." He lifted a hand and patted Campbell's shoulder. The hand stayed there.

Campbell leaned closer; his body tingled with nervous energy as he shifted his scrubs to adjust his growing enthusiasm.

Porter was the exact opposite of morose, and couldn't seem less defeated. Campbell had been mildly in love with him for several months now. He had dark, wavy hair with a thick pelt covering his arms and the base of his neck. He was a big man, strong and heavy, and would have been called a bear if he were not straight, married, and the father of three kids. The first time Campbell laid eyes on him, he felt this could be a suitable replacement, were he gay. Campbell would never love him with the same intensity as Sayen, but this man could give him a real relationship, or at least that was Campbell's fantasy. With those glasses and big teeth, Campbell could easily picture him on his living room carpet roughhousing with his boys.

"I'm thinking I should have gone to business school instead," Campbell said as he paid the cashier for both their meals.

They walked to the nearest table in silence and sat facing each other. Porter said, "Look at the bright side. You're in the one profession in this country that is not hopelessly corrupt, even if the drug and insurance companies who feed off our carcasses can't say the same."

Campbell ate a bit of Jell-O, and pushed the plate away.

"And don't you have some satisfaction," Porter continued, "knowing you're helping people in need, instead of churning out useless consumer goods?"

"I know, I know."

"Besides, it's too late now. You've spent years making yourself a damned good doctor. You can't throw that away."

"Can't I?"

"Come on, Cam, you just need a few weeks away. Go someplace relaxing, cut loose, get laid."

"Laid?" Campbell snapped. "Christ, that's the last thing I need." He realized that what spiked his anger was Porter calling him "Cam," which hadn't happened since Sayen.

Campbell swallowed down that ache and focused instead on Porter's heroism. He seemed a hero to Campbell because he worked predominantly in the burn unit, where the patients were in the most agony and the mortality rate was high.

The curious thing was that Porter had always treated Campbell as if he were also that same breed of hero, as if it simply never occurred to him that Campbell was a coward at heart.

"Sorry," he said with a masculine voice, mellow and singular, like a French horn rising above all the other instruments for a striking solo. "Only trying to cheer you up."

"What I need is a work environment that is real. This place is so dreary I sometimes think I'm losing my mind."

"Unreal? Perhaps," Porter said, glancing around the room. "But your affluent roots are showing. This austerity is a blessing. These rooms are built to a certain code and with unambiguous materials for a specific utility; no more and certainly no less. That scares rich people to death; they always demand more than they need. Our profession is much too austere for them. We reduce things from the material plane to mere symbolic conveniences so we can move beyond them. We free ourselves of luxuries in order to focus on what is meaningful, which is doing our job—saving lives. Seriously, no one can focus on healing the body or soul when their life is cluttered with material chaos, and the more expensive the stuff, the further away from reality we go."

Campbell stared into eyes the deepest shade of hazel he had ever seen, and wished he had the pluck to lean across the table and shut Porter up by planting a kiss over those full lips. He could easily imagine all the unisex fossils in the room raising their eyebrows in disgust. The question was, how would Porter react?

"Even the stupidest patients seem to understand that concept," Porter continued. "But the crowd who worships Parisian-designer clothes and vintage wines and first editions look down their noses at us because we renounce their world of class status based on objects-for-the-sake-of-objects. Don't get me wrong, there are some doctors who have gone over to the dark side, but they have lost their purpose. They look at us like we're hermits going into caves to contemplate, but that's only because they've been blinded by self-importance."

This was yet another example of Porter's heroic nature that Campbell didn't feel he measured up to. Rather than feeling better about himself, Campbell felt worse, much worse.

"Count your blessings, my friend. You and I have given up the material bullshit and become creatures of the spirit. We measure our existence by our deeds, not our belongings."

Campbell smiled shyly as he watched his colleague's delicate finger rub the bridge of his nose. Then Porter dropped his eyes, and began to fork his food into this mouth.

Campbell took a bite of fruit, imagining himself waking up next to Porter on a Saturday morning, with those three boys running into the bedroom and jumping on the bed, demanding their breakfast. Campbell's gut sunk a little deeper as his impossible desire burned into his brain tissue.

A moment later Porter dropped his fork and stood. Still caught in his fantasy, Campbell half expected him to pull Campbell out of his seat and into his arms, sweeping him from the room like Rhett Butler. A moment of silence stretched into an awkward pause as Campbell stared up into those sensual eyes. Finally Porter said, "Come on, I'll walk you back."

Campbell felt his gut drop an inch, and he looked down in disappointment, staring at the high-gloss polish of his friend's shoes. His eyes rode up the inseam of those green scrubs and stopped dead at crotch level. Campbell's X-ray vision kicked in to view, seeing that beautifully thick, three-piece set standing proud above dark hairy legs. A pressure built in his chest, and he reached for his inhaler, giving himself a pump.

Porter took Campbell by the arm, gently pulled him to his feet, and led him across the room. At the end of the hallway, Campbell began to plead for more time with this gentle man. At the same time he felt a growing loathing for Porter's wife. He searched his mind for something to say, some phrase that would give his friend a clue about what he so urgently needed, something to keep this man from leaving him alone to deal with his patients. Before anything came to mind, Porter opened the door to an examining room and pushed Campbell inside.

The room was empty and sterile. Campbell took a baby-step backward but stopped when he bumped into the examining table.

"I know what you need," Porter whispered, and he leaned into Campbell and locked his velvet lips to Campbell's mouth. Porter drew Campbell closer as his tongue forced its way between Campbell's lips.

Campbell felt his entire body liquefy as he drifted in a cloud of longing. He couldn't form a single thought. He could only feel this man's erotic touch. Reaching up to stroke those brawny shoulders, Campbell pushed back with his own tongue, becoming the aggressor. He pulled back only long enough to whisper, "This will ruin both our careers if someone walks in." At that moment, he didn't care. *Let them broadcast it on fucking CNN, as long as they don't stop us until after.*

Campbell found it endearing that Porter's hands shook while the big man pulled off Campbell's lab coat and green blouse. Both naked from the waist up, they embraced again, kissing passionately. The feel of that burly, pelt-covered skin was electric, sizzling all of Campbell's nerve endings. He was surprised and grateful that his kisses were returned with the same intensity.

Porter's hand enfolded his erection, and Campbell felt the pressure in his gut about to explode. He dropped his hands and cupped meaty wedges of butt.

"I have a condom," Porter grunted.

The full realization of what was happening blossomed in Campbell's mind. This would not be a quickie hand job, but the start of a real relationship. *My God*, he thought, *he's mine. All mine.* A feeling of numb joy passed through him. He didn't want to impede the passion, but he couldn't stop himself from asking, "What about your wife, your family?"

"What they don't know won't hurt them."

The fantasy collapsed like an exhaled breath. Campbell felt his whole being deflate, and so did his erection. He knew if he let this continue, he would become everything he had most hated for the last two years. His integrity was on the line, but so was his desperate need.

He placed his hands on Porter's chest and pushed, but the big man stopped him with a pleading gaze, while pulling at Campbell's scrubs.

In an act of surrender, Campbell kicked off his shoes and shimmied out of his pants and shorts. He leaned back on the examining table and hoisted his legs over Porter's shoulders. His dick remained limp and tears slid from the corners of his eyes as he begged for the big man to fuck him.

Later, as Campbell tugged on his underwear and scrubs, he no longer thought of Porter as heroic. As for himself, he grew afraid to turn his thoughts—his judgments—on his own behavior. His stomach turned leaden cartwheels, and he became sure he would vomit.

"Are you okay?" Porter said, pulling on his lab coat. He reached over and laid a calming hand on Campbell's shoulder.

Campbell stared at that hand. "I was such an idiot."

"It's alright. Next time will be better. We'll get a hotel room."

"Sure." Campbell glanced into those hazel eyes, so inviting, dragging him in. He knew the big man thought he was talking about what had just happened, but that wasn't so. Campbell was talking about something that happened two years ago. For the first time he understood, could clearly see into Sayen's soul and knew what he had let slip through his fingers.

When he walked back into the hallway, alone, he pulled his phone from his pocket and hit the speed dial. "Mother, my schedule just freed up. I can come to dinner."

CHAPTER TWENTY-ONE

MARILYN now lived in a Telegraph Hill high-rise, up a narrow street, which was always packed tight with cars parked on both side of it so that two drivers could scarcely squeeze past each other. Campbell found parking several blocks away at the bottom of the hill. Being raised in San Francisco, climbing hills was no issue for him. What he did find uncomfortable was the fact that he wore his tuxedo for the first time since the breakup. His shirt pinched at the neck, and his jacket squeezed at his shoulders. All that time at the gym, trying to work through his sorrow, had paid off. He knew, of course, that it was more than his ill-fitting tux; dressing for dinner was no longer a lifestyle he wanted to pursue.

He climbed slowly, taking the hill easy. He had progressed to an age where he thought it unseemly to arrive panting. Before entering her building, he took a moment to glance back down the hill. From this angle, he could see all the way to the bay. Even though the night was chilly, cooler air off the Pacific ripened into fog that smothered the water like a down quilt. Above, clouds hung in a loosely woven net, backlit by a waxing moon, which made the fog on the bay shine satiny, reminding him of bed and of how desperately he would rather be home asleep.

The African-American guard at the reception desk (who had sexy, muscular arms) was pleasant enough. Campbell already knew the number of Marilyn's apartment even though this was his first visit, so he simply said, "Hello," to the man as he walked to the elevator and pressed the button for the top floor.

The hallway was deserted, for the moment, and silent as a crypt. He hesitated outside her door—nervous and self-conscious, feeling as if he were about to cross into enemy territory—but then his hand lifted of its own accord and pushed the buzzer. The doorknob turned immediately, and the heavy, mahogany door swung open, as if she had been standing with her hand on the knob, waiting for him.

Her tinted hair looked pretty—it must have been recently waved—and made a charming blur around her eyes. It was her face and body that shocked him. She was a different person altogether—a shriveled mannequin with stick arms and legs, her withered face held a thick layer of makeup, and her sequined cocktail dress hung on her like a gunnysack, which only emphasized her lack of shape. But her eyes burned with that familiar arrogance, demanding that Campbell yield to the female prerogative. With unspoken words they cried, "I am still Marilyn. I am woman. I am your bitch-mother. I demand my biological rights."

"Merry Christmas, Mother," he mumbled, somewhat recovering from his astonishment.

"Please come in. I'm so pleased you could join me tonight."

The door swept full open, and she stepped aside to let him enter.

She had no doubt developed some sort of eating disorder. Campbell asked himself if, over these two years of hating her, even on that particular day she'd ripped his life away from him, would he have wished this on her?

The answer was no. Not because he was incapable of cruelty, but because there was simply no point in destroying her. Her sin was that she had fought Sayen and won, claiming Campbell for herself. Campbell had already robbed her of her prize by ignoring her for these two years. That was enough.

"Your eyes are just as brilliant blue as I remember," she said. "Two spheres cut from the sky on a sunny day."

"You writers are so full of it," he said with as much humor as he could muster.

She paused as he stood there. "Are those for me?"

Campbell looked to the bouquet of tulips in his hand. He held it out and then entered the apartment as she took her flowers.

He shed his overcoat as he glanced around the room and was stunned into silence for the second time in as many minutes. The living room was crammed with a mind-numbing number of belongings; the walls were concealed by paintings and sculptures. The room looked like a Sotheby's storeroom. In one corner of this white elephant sale stood a sparkling metal Christmas tree loaded down with unwieldy ornaments. The room was brightly lit, and the brightness offered a sort of sanctuary from loneliness. He could spend weeks or months here in a state of suspended insecurity, meditating on the multiplicity of objects.

These things were all familiar, and Campbell realized that she had shoehorned all the furniture and artwork from their spacious two-story family home into this five-room apartment. *She should not have sold the house,* he thought, *if she wanted to keep all this crap. And now that I'm here, she has all her belongings around her, all the things that matter to her are crammed into this sanctuary. She has a preoccupation with possession, and we all share that to some extent.*

Campbell realized that this bright room was not a sanctuary at all, but rather a place of shockingly vivid memories. He tried to swallow, but his throat was too dry. He took her hand and gave it a squeeze, then kissed her cheek. Had he done this even two months ago, it would have been loathsomely false. But since starting his affair with Porter, he had become one of them, one of the people who took, regardless of consequences. "Mother, it's really good to see you again. I'm so happy you called."

Her face lit up as he kissed her. He felt no revulsion or embarrassment, for the gesture meant, *You and I are cut from the same cloth. I am, it seems, your child after all.*

"Mother, you're so pale."

She sighed with amusement. "Dear, I don't get out much, now that I don't have a garden to tend."

"When was the last time you went shopping or out on the town?"

"Since I sold the house and moved here."

Fourteen months! She has gathered her wealth around her like a cloak, and is now waiting for what... death? There was a long silence. Campbell felt the terrible urge to say something, anything, but something had lodged in his throat, and he wasn't sure he could speak.

"I have everything I need right here, dear. Why should I go out?"

"Let's leave now. I'll take you to some swank restaurant for dinner." Suddenly he wanted to flee this high-rise. It seemed airless, as if it had become her Egyptian tomb. His body recoiled with its every nerve from the sight, smell, and feel of this place. He pulled his inhaler from his pocket and gave himself a blast.

Marilyn's hand suddenly gripped back with astonishing strength. "Don't be silly, dear. I've been cooking all day. And I have a surprise for you, the perfect gift."

It became clear that now that she had him here, she would not let him escape. He felt a drop of sweat break free of his underarm and slide down his flank.

She led him through a maze of furniture to a low loveseat littered with colorful silk cushions, too tiny to be useful but a perfect accent for the couch's fabric. Two Japanese scrolls hung on the wall behind the sofa: a snarling tiger and an immortal sitting under a tree, with three foot-long hairs growing from his chin. As Marilyn sat, she said, "Darling, should we open the champagne now, or would you prefer a cocktail before dinner?"

"I could use a martini."

"Perfect. Make mine vodka."

She had obviously had a couple already, he thought, and, of course, there is no way to water down a martini. But what the hell.

As he stepped to the bar and dropped ice into the shaker, her hands fumbled to light a cigarette. He glanced at the coffee table in front of her and noticed that the ashtray was full, and her color of lipstick marked all the stubs. Watching her smoke as he mixed, he thought she seemed even tougher than he remembered, yet at the same time so frail.

"It was sweet of you to come tonight. Tell me, dear, what was the engagement you broke tonight to be here?"

"It was nothing," Campbell said.

"I knew you were fibbing the moment you told me you had other plans. A mother knows."

How ironic that he fell into the cliché nonsense that his mother was the one person who understood him best. But no, he had opened himself to Sayen, who had known him to his core, knew every thought and desire. He had to stop himself. Letting his mind focus on Sayen, on what could have been his life, had long ago become torture. Time did nothing to lessen the pain. The only way to avoid pain was to avoid thinking about his losses.

"Yes, Mother, you have always had wonderful perception." He poured two double martinis and placed them on a tray, then set the still half-full shaker on the tray as well. He crossed the room, set the tray on the coffee table, and sat beside her. They toasted the season and drank, both taking half their drink in the first swallow. He topped them both off.

"Your father called me a few weeks ago," she said in a flat, underplayed tone.

"Oh?" Campbell managed to keep the surprise out of his voice. "Where is he?"

"Bangkok." She took another deep swallow and set her glass on the table with the kind of drama that made it seem as though she had said, "Antarctica."

"Jesus," Campbell blurted out. "How long has he lived there?"

"A year or a year and a half; does it matter? I often admire men for their uncanny ability to travel over thousands of miles of wilderness, pitch a tent on some godforsaken hillside, and call it home, and, of course, it would be home simply because that's the way a man's mind works. It's that pioneer spirit that built this country. Women need to put down roots, develop a sense of place and history, have cupboards to store the family china. If it had been up to the female species, we would have never made it as far as Plymouth Rock, let alone across the prairies. We can be transplanted only by a man dragging us by the hair, and if he resettles us, he must stick by us and care for us, because without his care our roots go into shock and wither."

Campbell gulped nearly a quarter of his martini to drown out the only question that had burned in his gut and kept him awake nights for two godforsaken years. Instead he asked, "Is he alone?"

In the moments of silence before she could answer, he felt the alcohol coming back on him with a rush. It was exhilarating, but it came too fast, making him sway slightly.

Marilyn held him with a level eye. "No. The point is, he has no intention of coming back to the States. We've lost him for good, I'm afraid. I've been abandoned, left for good. You certainly don't need me anymore, and your sister hates me. I've even lost all my friends. I'm like a moon torn from its planet's gravitational pull, floating aimlessly. Tell me, son, what am I doing here? I keep asking myself that question, and I have no answer."

The need to know mushroomed in Campbell's mind like an atomic explosion. He couldn't stop himself from asking, with a voice trembling and ominous, "But who is he with, Mother? Is it...." He managed to stop himself before he actually said the name and then took another gulp of vodka to steady himself.

She patted his knee. "No, dear. He's with some man of Thai origin that he no doubt met in a sleazy, Bangkok sex club. He is not with that man.... I must learn to say his name. He has a perfectly good name, and I can hardly pretend I don't know it."

Relief swept through Campbell like a sea swell. He polished off his drink and poured them both another.

"I know you think this whole messy breakup is my fault," she said. She held up a hand when he shook his head. "I don't blame you for thinking that. I know it's natural for you to take his side. But then, you've never had any children, so you have no idea how protective a parent can be."

Yes, he thought, *I don't have, and never will have, any children. You and your big mouth effectively robbed me of that as well.* But he saw tears trapped in her eyelashes, and his heart softened. He knew perfectly well he was equally to blame.

"Mother, it does no good to talk about the past. We are such a depressing pair. Let's eat."

She inched closer on the loveseat and squeezed his leg without speaking. They rose as one and crossed the room to the kitchen.

"Dear, open the champagne while I bring the food."

He checked the bottle's label, and his eyebrows lifted almost to his hairline. A '72 Dom Pérignon Brut! He uncorked the bottle and poured as she opened the oven door, donned oven mitts, and carried a casserole dish to the table. They toasted their health. The flavor opened up his head and tickled his taste buds—a delightfully pure ambrosia.

There was a bleak little pause. Campbell gave her shoulder an encouraging pat. "This is fantastic. How about I put another bottle on ice for after dinner?"

"That's an absolutely brilliant idea!" she said, and laughed gaily while swiping a tear from her cheek.

When he came back from the kitchen, he refilled their glasses, and they sat facing each other. They filled their plates with lobster and leeks, and began to eat. He pretended not to notice that she merely pushed food around her plate. Occasionally she would lift a forkful of lobster to her mouth, but the instant before she was about to take a bite, she would suddenly remember something to say, and she would start the conversation down another path while lowering her food back to her plate.

He smiled at her, feeling a warm concern for her health and a desire to encourage her to eat, but it could have been sentimental stimulation from the alcohol. They were both flying pretty high.

She said, "I think I will move back to my family's home in Virginia. I dread it, but it's what's best."

"Why do you dread it?"

"Because it means moving in with my sister, and we loathe each other. She was always jealous of Blake. He was a real looker back in the day, and he was so much better looking than her Walter. And I confess, I lorded it over her, a bit. I was proud of your father; who wouldn't have been?"

"But she knows Dad and you have split up, right?"

"Oh yes. I phoned her as soon as it happened. I couldn't endure the shame of her finding out from someone else, and she has the uncanniest way of discovering these types of beastly embarrassments. I could hear her gloating over the phone. Walter was homely and boring as a mud fence, but at least he stuck with her until she put him in the ground. I suppose it's karma that I'll have to endure her reveling now."

Campbell cuffed the corner of his mouth with his napkin. "I'm sure she's unhappy that this all happened. You're just imagining her gloating."

"Of course I denied being upset over it—you know me!—and told her I was glad to be rid of him, and that I was blissfully happy to be single again. I had a line of suitors to choose from."

"Mother!"

Marilyn lifter her glass and sipped her champagne. "She saw right through me, of course, and rightfully so. I felt so appallingly embarrassed."

"Well if that's how you feel, then stay here. Don't move back to a place you'll be miserable."

She sipped more of her drink. "Darling, you've always been a delightfully simple creature. There are things you endure for the sake of family, because enduring them is better than having nothing. Besides, underneath all that jealousy, your aunt does love me. She is two years older than I, and she cared for me while we were growing up. She loved me fiercely up until the time I met your father. That kind of love doesn't fade away; it digs in deeper. No, I must go back. It's all I have to cling to now."

They both sat frozen for what turned into an awkward minute.

She finally said, "If I'm to move, I suppose I should make an effort to send all your father's clothes to Good Will. He left most of his things behind."

More silence.

"I mean," she continued after a sip of Brut, "I won't feel any amount of closure until I do. You do understand, don't you?"

"Yes, Mother. I understand perfectly."

"I've already sold most of his personal things, even his Bentley. And I've sent him all the money. God knows he has no income now. But for some silly reason I held on to his clothes."

Campbell took another bite and chewed in silence before washing it down with wine.

"You know," she continued, once he set his glass down and she could stare deeply into his eyes, all the way to his soul, "you and I—it's funny—we are in the same sinking ship now. We both have so much, yet so little."

"Mother—"

"Darling," she interrupted, "I need to ask you something—it's not that I'm trying to pry, but I need to know."

"Okay, Mother, ask away."

Swaying slightly, she regarded him earnestly but dimly, as though she were peering up at him, fishlike, through a pond of murky vodka. "I know you have not had a steady boyfriend since... well, since that night. What I need to know is, has there been anyone you felt something for? Anyone who you wanted to love?"

He knew then that she had had him followed, spied on. It felt like a violation, something dirty. He felt he should have been surprised, but he wasn't. A coldness crept into his chest, and he glanced at the front door, wanting a quick getaway. "Mother, I'll clear the table and help wash the dishes."

He started to rise, but she reached across the table and laid her hand on one of his. "Sit down, you goose. I have a maid that will clean everything in the morning."

"In that case, I think it's getting late. We can open that second bottle of wine some other time. Perhaps New Year's?"

"I'm going to take your refusing to answer my question as an emphatic no. You have felt no love for anybody since Sayen."

There, damn it, she had said his name. Why? What was the point in bringing all that up?

Campbell heard a clicking across the living room, and a moment later the front door swung open. He watched a middle-age, Hispanic woman enter and shut the door. She was dressed in a nurse's uniform. He was suddenly aware of Marilyn saying, "I had to know the truth before I gave you your Christmas present."

The nurse crossed the room and stood beside the table. "Hello. I'm Deloris. I've come to put Mrs. Reardon to bed." She placed a small purse-like bag on the table and unzipped it, opening it up like a set of butterfly wings to display a hypodermic and the ampoules.

Campbell rose to his feet. "I should be going."

"No need to run right out," Deloris said. "This takes a little time to make her drowsy. You can keep her company for another half hour."

"Campbell," Marilyn said, ignoring Deloris. She held out a pale-yellow envelope. "This is my gift to you, son."

Campbell reached across the table and took the envelope, feeling guilty for receiving a present when he'd brought nothing but flowers.

"I see you have been a bad girl again, Mrs. Reardon," Deloris said, glancing down at Marilyn's full plate. "You must eat something."

Again, Marilyn ignored her, as if Deloris were some sad illusion in Campbell's head. "Open it now," Marilyn said.

Campbell tore open the envelope as he sat back in his chair. Inside he found a single slip of paper with an address. He read it twice before he realized it was an address for a Tunisian town he had never heard of.

He glanced across the table, but Marilyn was no longer staring at him. Her eyes were now fixed on the needle in Deloris's hand. "Mother, what is this?"

"It's a clinic where you will find Sayen. Your father gave that address to me and asked that I send him money. I want you to go there and meet with him."

A long pause.

"I don't understand."

"Darling, I'm giving him back to you, or you back to him. Whichever. I want you to be happy, to get on with your life. Go to him."

"Mother, I can't."

"You'll either find love or closure." She pulled her gaze away from the needle as Deloris took her arm and rubbed a spot with a little cotton ball. Marilyn stared into his soul again. "Dear, this is the last thing I will ever ask of you. Do this for me. And for your sake, I hope it's not too late. Go there with an open heart. Don't end up like me."

Campbell rose to his feet again. "Mother—"

"Don't worry one bit about me, son. One of the first things a mother teaches her daughters is how to be a good loser. It's one of our most important qualities. I'll be fine."

After a suitable pause, she said with a tone of utter indifference, "Goodbye, my darling." Marilyn looked back at the needle.

He reached across the table and took her hand. She didn't respond. She only saw the bright needle as it pressed to her arm.

Campbell knew then that the last traces of the woman who had stolen Sayen from him had vanished, and with her disappearance, so went the last of his animosity for her. Now his only abhorrence left was for Sayen. That had been the tragic bond between the three of them, hate. But as Campbell ambled down Telegraph Hill to his car, he realized that his hate for Sayen had vanished as well.

CHAPTER TWENTY-TWO

BLAKE rode in the backseat of a Bangkok taxi down a main shopping-district boulevard. The traffic was its normal stop and crawl, and he began to worry that he would be late for the plane. Although Thailand is predominately Buddhist and Muslim, the department stores were all weighed down with gaudy Christmas decorations—reindeer and Santas in sleds slung across the street on cables, and palm trees lit up with twinkling lights like Christmas trees swayed before a sultry wind. Shoppers thronged the sidewalks, their eyes reflecting, like polished stones, the cynical glitter of the Yuletide. In the lean years after a tsunami devastated the southern islands, there had been little money for luxuries; the shops and restaurants were empty, people scarcely had enough money for rice. In the last year, however, the tourists had returned in droves. The merchants were predicting a good year. People had less money than before, but they had enough. Even the horde of young hustlers (identifiable at once to Blake's experienced eyes) who stood posing on the street corners seemed to wear newer, more fashionable clothing.

Though Blake now enjoyed a quiet relationship with a middle-aged Thai man, he would never allow himself to sneer at these boys working the bars and streets. They may be uneducated and mercenary, but they were out and proud and making a living by giving pleasure. He felt gratified to be among them, almost indecently gleeful to stand among the ranks of this most flamboyant minority. He caught the notice of one tawny-skinned creature with haunting bright eyes. The boy waved and Blake waved back, with a warm, appreciative smile. Yes, Thailand was called the land of smiles, and Blake understood why.

They have no idea how lucky they are, he thought, *these lovely street-boys*, but Blake knew all too well, having lived both sides of that dividing plane. He had abandoned the majority, and now he felt completely alive, and even more so today because in another hour, his son would touch down at Suvarnabhumi Airport, and they would finally start a reconciliation.

"I am alive," he mumbled to himself. He said it again, louder and with much feeling. The driver didn't even turn his head. No doubt he was used to wacky Farangs—Westerners.

Blake was not the least bit embarrassed. He felt energy surging through his capillaries, a delightful, warm-blooded hunger for life. His old, beat-up carcass had nearly died, he had almost given up, but now he knew there was still much life in front of him. The sleek youths on the corners saw him, no doubt, only as a doddering cash cow, yet he still felt a distant kinship with the strength of their bodies, their loins, their spirit.

It would be so easy to have one. Twenty bucks would buy him the pick of the litter. But he didn't want their bodies. He was quite happy with his middle-aged lover. What he wanted was merely to rejoice in his own body, to love, and to be loved.

He checked his watch, again, not wanting to miss Campbell's landing. He desperately wanted to see his son's face as he walked up the ramp. *Yes, to love and be loved.*

CHAPTER TWENTY-THREE

WITH only twenty minutes notice, Sayen had prepared as best he could for another flight into the Libyan war zone. Four hundred and fifty miles can be no great distance in a plane—even a dilapidated, four-seater Cessna Skycatcher—or it can be from where you are to the end of the earth. On a night flight like this one, it all depended on a variety of things—the depth of the darkness, the height of the clouds, the speed of the wind, the brightness of the moon, and if the enemy was feeling trigger happy.

There had been a skirmish that day in Surt, a city east of Tripoli. Tanks had pounded the insurgents, and the bloodied rebels were regrouping in the hills south of the battlefield. A principal member of the rebellion needed medical attention, so once again Sayen was drawn into the fight. He operated a clinic in Tunisia, near the border with Libya, giving medical aid to the thousands of refugees fleeing his homeland. But as the fighting escalated, he found himself spending more and more time giving aid to the combatants inside Libya.

He wasn't too concerned with his own safety, but he hated leaving Halle and the baby alone in, what was to them, a foreign environment.

His clinic was a somewhat barren little structure on the beach overlooking the Mediterranean. It had started as a place of small hopes and small successes, but had grown into a treasure for people fleeing the war. He felt proud of his contribution to his people, and prouder still that Halle, when not caring for their son, also helped in whatever way presented itself.

As he strapped himself into the co-pilot seat, he did not feel the least bit heroic. It didn't feel patriotic or romantic, either. It was work, a job to be done at one o'clock in the morning with sleep in his eyes and half a grumble on his lips.

Ruta, the pilot, reached for the key. The engine spluttered a strangled cough, and the propeller came alive. In the cockpit dome light, Sayen watched Ruta run down his preflight checklist. Ruta had grown up in Zimbabwe, and his skin was the color of old copper. His eyes were dark and spaced wide apart, and they were incapable of hiding his palpable arrogance. Ruta and Sayen seldom spoke on these night journeys. Ruta's mastery of the sky was beyond reproach, and he never needed any help in finding their destination. They were close friends and often engaged in long, enjoyable conversations, but never on these flights. These missions were all business.

Ruta eased the throttle forward. The motor whine grew deafening, and the plane lurched down the dirt runway. They passed splashes of crimson light from crude-oil torches set alongside the strip, gathering speed as they met the wind head on.

They lifted into the sky, and night enveloped them entirely. Ahead of them lay a strange mixture of grasslands, scrub, desert sand, and age-old mountains as stark and grim as craters on the moon.

They flew high and as swift as the plane was capable. Time and distance slipped smoothly past the wingtips. Sayen was relaxed, but too wired to sleep. For a time, he felt out of touch with the earth, leaving him in a unique living space filled with stars and the constant groan of the Skycatcher's engine. He felt as if in a trance until the plane nosed earthward, and he saw the wavering crude-oil torches outlining no more than a narrow runway—a thin scar on a vast wilderness.

They circled the field once, watching the flares yield to the wind, gauging how strong and from which direction the breeze flowed. Ruta pulled back on the throttle and held the plane's nose on the beacons until the land rushed to meet them and the wheels touched earth. As they came to a halt, Ruta cut the engine and relaxed in his seat. His job was done for the night, while Sayen's was about to begin.

As he climbed from the cockpit, Sayen heard the excited voices of men drifting across the runway, sounding like the thin bleating of sheep. He saw a band of figures approaching before the dancing flares. He could see from their dress that they were all rebels in this ragtag army. No one seemed to be in charge. Ruta handed him his medical bag, but made no move to exit the plane himself. Sayen was led away by the excited group, and he knew his friend would stay and guard the plane for however long this job took, be it a few hours or a few days.

A short bull of a man approached Sayen in the uncertain light. His face was pockmarked under a patch of graying hair, and his weary eyes held Sayen's with a confident air. "You made good time."

"All part of the platinum service," Sayen said. He had dealt with this man, Momar, before. They both had developed a firm respect for each other.

Momar wore a gray, blood-stained shirt and loose military trousers. He spoke apologetically, as if Sayen were a dignitary visiting from another, more glamorous civilization, who would certainly find the conditions less than what he should expect.

"Follow me. I have three injured men, and one of them is my right-hand man. We have some supplies, so let me know whatever you need."

Sayen nodded, staring into that thick, sun-beaten face. "Can you have some food and tea taken to my pilot?"

"It won't be good, but he can have his fill."

Momar led Sayen up a rocky hill to the rebel encampment. In the weak light, Sayen saw the rebel camp in all its bleak and courageous isolation—a brick building with a roof of corrugated iron surrounded by a handful of tents and pickup trucks. Weary men, hollow-bellied and dispirited, sprawled in the dust. Sayen saw no sign of women or children. This camp was without human warmth, a place without even laughter.

Inside the only structure, a hurricane lamp with a soot-smeared chimney stood on a shelf, lighting a single bleak room that had three men lying on a dirt floor. Sayen lifted the lamp and moved to the first patient.

In that crude yellow light, he saw that there was nothing to be done for Momar's right-hand man, who had been shot twice, chest and gut, with high caliber bullets. Sayen was surprised he had lasted as long as he did. Even if they could get him to a modern hospital, he certainly would be dead before morning. He gave the man a shot of painkiller, and moved on.

Sayen took Momar aside and explained there was nothing to be done for his right-hand man except to keep him as comfortable as possible for the few minutes he had left. Momar's face drooped into a frown that Sayen suspected would not lift anytime soon.

The second patient had bandages covering half his face, and his right pant leg had been ripped away to reveal a bullet wound four inches above the knee. Fortunately, the bullet had come from a small caliber rifle and had missed the bone and the major artery. This one he could save.

He told Momar that he needed hot water and a bit of soap, and then he moved the light closer to the man's face. He began to unwrap the makeshift bandage, revealing a hideous burn. Sayen was somewhat amazed that this man could endure such a large and excruciating burn in silence. *They have already sedated him,* he thought, *or perhaps this is a man who has had much experience with pain.*

The patient mumbled a request for a smoke. Sayen dug into his pockets for the pack he kept for this purpose, placed a cigarette between the man's lips, and lit it. He tried to shake off a wave of sleepiness, but it was futile. A moment later, Momar returned carrying a mug of strong tea.

"Drink this, brother, while I fetch your water."

The drink opened Sayen's eyes, both from the vile flavor and from the sweetness, which was sure to give him a sugar high. His first thought was to spit it out, but he swallowed while scrunching up his face. *This stuff will dissolve my fillings*, he thought, but he was grateful for it anyway. No matter how bad it tasted, he needed it.

With the bandage removed, he lifted the lantern close to the man's face. A burn covered half of the face, and much of the man's hair and beard had been scorched away. The other half of the face was blackened with blood and dirt. Sayen leaned close to examine the eye on the burnt half. The skin around it was red and blistered, but the watery eye seemed both fine and vaguely familiar.

The patient blew out a stream of smoke. "So you finally came home, brother."

For a moment, all Sayen heard was a voice from his past calling to him, a drunken voice filled with lust. Sayen could feel his throat tighten. "Mahmud?"

Momar lumbered up to place a pan of boiling water beside Sayen. He fanned his fingers for a moment, then dropped a clean towel and a bar of soap beside the pan.

Sayen's brother managed a lopsided grin, then sucked in another lungful of smoke, and exhaled through his nose.

Sayen's memory shuttled backward to the days of his childhood at his family home—days when adoration for Mahmud had colored every part of his being. Those were days of deeply felt joys and heavy-scented shame, days of a lust and a love that eventually stripped Sayen of his family and his culture.

"Mahmud, I'm going to give you a shot of painkiller, then clean and dress your wounds. In the morning, I'll fly you back to my clinic in Tunisia to care for you."

"No, brother, you must leave me here. I will never abandon my people."

His brother's words sounded like an accusation. He wanted to defend himself, especially since Mahmud was the cause of that abandonment, but he dug into his medical bag, choosing to do his job with as little emotion as he could manage.

Sayen took a pair of surgical tongs and placed a syringe, forceps, and scalpel into the steaming water. He washed his hands with the cake of soap, wiped his hands dry on the towel, and used the tongs to pull the syringe from the pan. Holding a vile of morphine up to the lamplight, he stuck the needle through the rubber stopper, drew a syringeful, thumbed the plunger back to the proper dose, and gave his brother an injection.

Mahmud closed his eyes, his mind no doubt drifting to a far-away void. But before he lost consciousness, he mumbled, "I'm sorry, brother. Forgive me."

The ball of cactus in Sayen's gut reeled, doing a slow rotation. He wasn't exactly sure if his brother's plea for forgiveness was for now or for their past, but he desperately wanted to believe it was not for now. He felt there must have been a hundred things for him to say before Mahmud lost consciousness, but he couldn't think of a single one. He reached up and took the stub of cigarette from his brother's mouth and ground it out on the earthen floor.

Sayen first worked on the bleeding leg, digging the bullet from the flesh, cleaning, stitching, and bandaging the wound. The sight of blood still sickened him, but he swallowed down his panic and worked without stopping until he had the leg bandaged. As he moved back to clean the facial injury, he felt the tingle of pride because he knew he had worked fastidiously under these impossible conditions to save the one person he had always loved above all others.

Yet, as he painstakingly cleaned his brother's face, he began to recognize that his feelings for Mahmud had changed. No, changed was the wrong interpretation, he realized. The truth was, what he had always thought of as a profound love for Mahmud had been eclipsed by a truer, richer love for Campbell. He felt like a child comprehending that stars were farther away than clouds. That understanding brought both hurt and joy.

By the time Sayen had finished dressing the burn, his tea had gone stone-cold. He drank it anyway, needing something to give him a jolt. He moved on to the third patient, and found the man already dead.

CHAPTER TWENTY-FOUR

ON A wide sloping beach, tucked into coconut palms, stood a white building with a large red cross and a red crescent on the wall. It had a covered porch, and a line of Muslim women holding infants snaked out the door and along the wall. Wrapped in long dresses and headscarves, the women fanned their crying children.

Inside the clinic, Sayen stood beside a table where he was sewing up a wound on a child's leg. He wore a white smock and jeans, and the early morning heat had brought a sheen of sweat to his forehead. The child was crying and reaching for its mother, who stood waiting by the door. She spoke to him in her native tongue, trying to soothe the boy's fears. On the far side of the room, a pregnant woman lay on a table with her knees elevated, in the early stages of labor. A native nurse, also dressed in a white smock, attended her.

Sayen lifted his head, glanced out the large open windows, and saw Halle sitting on the beach with waves swirling over her feet. Between her spread legs teetered a two-year-old, naked toddler. He smiled, thinking for the millionth time what a fine mother she had become. The roar of an engine seized his attention. He watched as a jeep raced up and parked near the clinic. The driver was dressed in a military uniform, but the passenger was a civilian. Sayen's heart nearly stopped as he watched Campbell Reardon unfold from the jeep, lift two bags from the back, carry them to the porch, and deposit them by the front door.

Islamic music was playing from an old CD player, but Sayen was beyond hearing anything.

Campbell stepped inside as the jeep roared away. As Campbell entered the operating room, Sayen saw only his eyes—so clear, so defenseless. Sayen's memory had drawn his ex-lover many times, but for some reason he had always sketched him younger, with more of the vitality of youth.

Campbell moved close to the table where Sayen worked on the child's leg. Campbell's shoulders looked wider than Sayen remembered, more filled out. But as their eyes drilled into each other, those shoulders sagged, and his expression turned into a comical blend of fatigue and delight. Sayen's throat grew dry as his pulse went haywire.

Sayen had to refocus on the boy's leg, making another stitch. He swallowed to make his voice work. "Dr. Reardon I presume. How did you find us?" he said without looking up.

"I visited my father in Bangkok. He told me that after you completed your residency and became a doctor, you came here to run this clinic by begging, borrowing, and stealing medical supplies from the World Health Organization."

Sayen chuckled as he made another perfect stitch. "Blake deals with the W.H.O.; we only treat patients." Holding his hands still, he glanced up into Campbell's face again. He held Campbell's stare for a moment, then bent his head over the child's leg again and continued to meticulously sew the wound.

"So you finally came home to your own people. I'm proud of you, but didn't anyone tell you there was a revolution going on? I was shot at on my way from the airport!"

"My people require help," Sayen said with a melancholy smile. "They need me."

"Doctors Without Borders," Campbell said in a soft voice. "I didn't think you'd go through with it."

"Easiest thing I ever did. And Halle's turned into a damned fine mother. But you were wrong, she's not the best of your family.

Blake made this possible. All this"—he waved an arm at the room—
"is his Bentley."

Campbell studied the clean and orderly room. He noted that it
had an impressive amount of modern equipment for such a
backwater clinic. "It's a pity I never got to drive that car before he
sold it."

"At least we made love in it. We'll always have that."

Campbell grew silent for a long time. Sayen saw only
Campbell's eyes again, staring back at him out of some private,
lonely place.

"How did your visit with Blake go?" Sayen asked as he
finished the stitching and began to tie a knot.

"He and his partner seem happy. What about you? Is there
someone in your life?"

"Oh yes. Didn't Blake tell you?"

"No. All he said was I should come here and see you."

"It's funny, I was always the taker. I gave a little sex and took
everything you and Blake had to offer. But now I'm head over heels
with someone who takes everything I have: my time, my money, my
love. And he gives nothing back. He barely speaks a dozen words to
me. Karma."

Campbell turned his head, staring out the window as Sayen
finished the knot.

"I'd like you to meet him," Sayen said.

Campbell backed away, shaking his head. "Bad idea."

Sayen swabbed the child's wound with antiseptic. "Seriously,
you'll like him. He's sometimes hard to take because he's in the
middle of his terrible twos, but he's adorable. His name is Campbell
Beckham Reardon Jr., and he's our son. Halle is out there teaching
him how to swim."

Campbell stared out the window, studying his sister at the
water's edge. A toddler came into view. "Our son? Did you two get
married?"

Sayen placed a bandage over the boy's leg and began to secure it. "Ours, as in yours and mine, Cam. I forged your name on the adoption papers. Marilyn didn't tell you?"

Campbell whirled around, eyes wide, looking like Bambi caught in the high beams. A visible shudder ran through him, like sparks of electricity jolting every muscle. "Did I hear that right? Our son? Yours and mine? Are you pulling my chain?"

Sayen savored the words and their sounds like the taste of a Château Margaux Cru Classé. *Our son.* "Marilyn didn't tell you?"

Campbell shrugged. "She and I don't speak much these days, so no, she didn't tell me. Neither did Blake, the bastard."

"She was the one who helped with the adoption," Sayen said, "although she was gritting her teeth the whole time. Anyway, trot out there and meet him while I finish up in here. Halle and I can catch you up over dinner. I assume you're staying a few days, right? I mean, you didn't come all this way, after two years, just to spit in my eye and leave?"

Campbell started to move to take Sayen in his arms but stopped, shaking his head, still stunned. "I never figured you would go through with this clinic stuff. I mean, charity work in a war zone? And raising a child?"

Sayen pulled the rubber gloves from his hands and gave the boy on the table a loving pat on the shoulder. "I like it here, and my people respect me."

"It must get desperately lonely."

"I've learned a trick to cope with loneliness. Whenever it gets so bad that I want to blow my brains out, I picture our picnic on the beach when I realized how deeply I loved you, and how I felt when we made love in the Bentley. Then I remember how I lost you a few hours later, and I realize that if I can survive that, I can survive anything."

They hugged, folding into each other. Sayen's face pressed into Campbell's soft, warm neck, so close that he absorbed some of Campbell into his own chest.

"Hard to believe you've changed so much," Campbell whispered.

They pulled apart and Sayen asked, "Enough to earn back your respect?"

"Don't think I've forgiven you. Some things can never be the same."

Sayen gave an understanding nod. He heard the crying of children in the waiting room, where suffering still lived and people struggled to move from one moment to the next, that world that he was now recklessly ignoring. He put his arms around the child, lifted the boy, and turned toward the doorway. He began to blink his eyes rapidly, holding back tears. "I've got sweat in my eyes."

Campbell pulled a white monogrammed handkerchief from his pocket and dabbed Sayen's forehead and cheeks. Then he tucked the cloth into Sayen's pocket, patting Sayen on the shoulder. Sayen froze, staring at that beautiful monogrammed stitching on the pristine white cotton.

Campbell scanned the tiny clinic again, eyeing the line of women and children waiting for treatment. "I'll scrub up and give you a hand. That way you can finish early, and we can both take our son for a swim."

Sayen nodded, not trusting himself to speak.

Campbell approached the room's only sink, rolled up his sleeves, and began to wash. "This place is totally inadequate, with too many patients for one M.D., which is why D.W.B. sent me here. With a little reorganization and a second treatment room, we can really make an impact here."

Still holding the child to his chest, Sayen glanced up and met Campbell's eyes. They shared a tender moment, and Sayen handed the boy to his mother and led the next patient into the room.

At sunset, Sayen and Halle sat on the beach, dripping seawater and staring out over an iridescent sea. Campbell and his son swam together, and Sayen saw their uncovered heads, black and golden, above the water. He watched them rise out of the surf with the child perched on Campbell's shoulders, both naked, unshy, beautiful, and full of grace. They were laughing at the sheer joy of living, and Sayen admired the naked man he loved walking out of the sea.

ALAN CHIN enjoyed a twenty-year career working his way from computer programmer to Director of Software Engineering, but he lost interest in computer science when he began writing fiction. He walked away from corporate America in 1999 and never looked back. Since then he has traveled to over forty countries, scuba dived the Great Barrier Reef, tracked black rhino in the Serengeti, and dined in most of the capitals of Europe. Oh yes, and he's published four gay-themed novels and two screenplays.

In addition to writing, Alan is making a name for himself as a literary critic for several online publications which include: Examiner.com GLBT Literature column, *Queer Magazine Online*, and the Lambda Literary web site. In 2007, *QBliss* magazine awarded their Pride In Literature award to Alan for his debut novel. In 2010, Alan's novel, *The Lonely War*, swept the Rainbow Literary Awards, taking top honors in four categories: Best Fiction, Best Historical, Best Characters, and Best Setting.

Alan currently spends half of the year traveling the globe and the other half writing at his home in Palm Springs, California.

You can visit Alan's web site at http://alanchin.net and his writers blog at http://alanchinwriter.blogspot.com. You can also e-mail Alan at Alanhchin@aol.com.

Also from ALAN CHIN

BUTTERFLY'S CHILD

ALAN CHIN

http://www.dreamspinnerpress.com

Also from ALAN CHIN

MATCH MAKER

ALAN CHIN

http://www.dreamspinnerpress.com

Also from ALAN CHIN

http://www.dreamspinnerpress.com

Made in United States
Orlando, FL
22 March 2026

79558922R00118